TIMEQUAKE

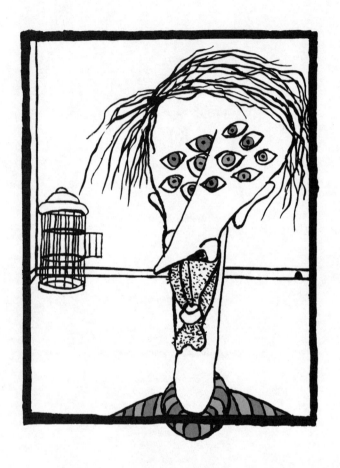

Out-of-print science fiction writer Kilgore Trout

in Cohoes, New York, in 1975, having learned of

the death of his estranged son, Leon, in a Swedish

shipyard, having given his parakeet, "Cyclone Bill,"

his freedom, and about to become a vagabond.

TIMEQUAKE

KURT VONNEGUT

G. P. Putnam's Sons
New York

Published by G. P. Putnam's Sons
Publishers Since 1838
a member of Penguin Putnam Inc.
200 Madison Avenue
New York, NY 10016
Published simultaneously in Canada

The text of this book is set in Fournier MT.

Library of Congress Cataloging-in-Publication Data

Vonnegut, Kurt.
Timequake / Kurt Vonnegut.
p.   cm.
ISBN 0-399-13737-8
ISBN 0-399-13898-6 (Limited Edition)
I.   Title.
PS3572.O5T56   1997   97-14508 CIP
813'.54—dc21

Printed in the United States of America
5   7   9   10   8   6
This book is printed on acid-free paper. ∞

Book design by Claire Naylon Vaccaro

In memory of Seymour Lawrence,

a romantic and great publisher

of curious tales told with ink

on bleached and flattened wood pulp

All persons, living and dead, are purely coincidental.

PROLOGUE

Ernest Hemingway in 1952 published in *Life* magazine a long short story called *The Old Man and the Sea*. It was about a Cuban fisherman who hadn't caught anything for eighty-four days. The Cuban hooked an enormous marlin. He killed it and lashed it alongside his little boat. Before he could get it to shore, though, sharks bit off all the meat on the skeleton.

I was living in Barnstable Village on Cape Cod when the story appeared. I asked a neighboring commercial fisherman what he thought of it. He said the hero was an idiot. He should have hacked off the best chunks of meat and put them in the bottom of the boat, and left the rest of the carcass for the sharks.

It could be that the sharks Hemingway had in mind were critics who hadn't much liked his first novel in ten years, *Across the River and into the Trees*, published two years earlier. As far as I know, he never said so. But the marlin could have been that novel.

And then I found myself in the winter of 1996 the creator of a novel which did not work, which had no point, which had never wanted to be written in the first place. *Merde!* I had spent nearly a decade on that un-grateful fish, if you will. It wasn't even fit for shark chum.

I had recently turned seventy-three. My mother made it to fifty-two, my father to seventy-two. Hemingway almost made it to sixty-two. I had lived too long! What was I to do?

Answer: Fillet the fish. Throw the rest away.

This I did in the summer and autumn of 1996. Yesterday, November 11th of that year, I turned seventy-four. Seventy-four!

Johannes Brahms quit composing symphonies when he was fifty-five. Enough! My architect father was sick and tired of architecture when he was fifty-five. Enough! American male novelists have done their best work by then. Enough! Fifty-five is a long time ago for me now. Have pity!

My great big fish, which stunk so, was entitled *Timequake*. Let us think of it as *Timequake One*. And let us think of this one, a stew made from its best parts mixed with thoughts and experiences during the past seven months or so, as *Timequake Two*.

Hokay?

The premise of *Timequake One* was that a timequake, a sudden glitch in the space-time continuum, made everybody and everything do exactly what they'd done during a past decade, for good or ill, a second time. It was déjà vu that wouldn't quit for ten long years. You couldn't complain about life's being nothing but old stuff, or ask if just you were going nuts or if *everybody* was going nuts.

There was absolutely nothing you could say during the rerun, if you hadn't said it the first time through the decade. You couldn't even save your own life or that of a loved one, if you had failed to do that the first time through.

. . . . .

I had the timequake zap everybody and everything in an instant from February 13th, 2001, back to February 17th, 1991. Then we all had to get back to 2001 the hard way, minute by minute, hour by hour, year by year, betting on the wrong horse again, marrying the wrong person again, getting the clap again. You name it!

Only when people got back to when the timequake hit did they stop being robots of their pasts. As the old science fiction writer Kilgore Trout said, "Only when free will kicked in again could they stop running obstacle courses of their own construction."

Trout doesn't really exist. He has been my alter ego in several of my other novels. But most of what I have chosen to preserve from *Timequake One* has to do with his adventures and opinions. I have salvaged a few of the thousands of stories he wrote between 1931, when he was fourteen, and 2001, when he died at the age of eighty-four. A hobo for much of his life, he died in luxury in the Ernest Hemingway Suite of the writers' retreat Xanadu in the summer resort village of Point Zion, Rhode Island. That's nice to know.

His very first story, he told me as he was dying, was set in Camelot, the court of King Arthur in Britain: Merlin the Court Magician casts a spell that allows him to equip the Knights of the Round Table with Thompson submachine guns and drums of .45-caliber dumdums.

Sir Galahad, the purest in heart and mind, familiarizes himself with this new virtue-compelling appliance. While doing so, he puts a slug through the Holy Grail and makes a Swiss cheese of Queen Guinevere.

. . . . .

Here is what Trout said when he realized that the ten-year rerun was over, that he and everybody else were suddenly obligated to think of new stuff to do, to be creative again: "Oh, Lordy! I am much too old and experienced to start playing Russian roulette with free will again."

Yes, and I myself was a character in *Timequake One,* making a cameo appearance at a clambake on the beach at the writers' retreat Xanadu in the summer of 2001, six months after the end of the rerun, six months after free will kicked in again.

I was there with several fictitious persons from the book, including Kilgore Trout. I was privileged to hear the old, long-out-of-print science fiction writer describe for us, and then demonstrate, the special place of Earthlings in the cosmic scheme of things.

So now my last book is done, with the exception of this preface. Today is November 12th, 1996, about nine months, I would guess, from its publication date, from its emergence from the birth canal of a printing press. There is no rush. The gestation period for a baby Indian elephant is more than twice that long.

The gestation period for a baby opossum, friends and neighbors, is twelve days.

I have pretended in this book that I will still be alive for the clambake in 2001. In chapter 46, I imagine myself as still alive in 2010. Sometimes I say I'm in 1996, where I really am, and sometimes I say I am in the midst of a rerun following a timequake, without making clear distinctions between the two situations.

I must be nuts.

TIMEQUAKE

1

Call me Junior. My six grown kids do. Three are adopted nephews, three are my own. They call me Junior behind my back. They think I don't know that.

I say in speeches that a plausible mission of artists is to make people appreciate being alive at least a little bit. I am then asked if I know of any artists who pulled that off. I reply, "The Beatles did."

It appears to me that the most highly evolved Earthling creatures find being alive embarrassing or much worse. Never mind cases of extreme discomfort, such as idealists' being crucified. Two important women in my life, my mother and my only sister, Alice, or Allie, in Heaven now, hated life and said so. Allie would cry out, "I give up! I give up!"

The funniest American of his time, Mark Twain, found life for himself and everybody else so stressful when he was in his seventies, like me, that he wrote as follows: "I have never wanted any released friend of mine restored to life since I reached manhood." That is in an essay on the sudden death of his daughter Jean a few days earlier. Among those he wouldn't have resurrected were Jean, and another daughter, Susy, and his beloved wife, and his best friend, Henry Rogers.

Twain didn't live to see World War One, but still he felt that way.

Jesus said how awful life was, in the Sermon on the Mount: "Blessed are they that mourn," and "Blessed are the meek," and "Blessed are they which do hunger and thirst after righteousness."

Henry David Thoreau said most famously, "The mass of men lead lives of quiet desperation."

So it is not one whit mysterious that we poison the water and air and topsoil, and construct ever more cunning doomsday devices, both industrial and military. Let us be perfectly frank for a change. For practically everybody, the end of the world can't come soon enough.

My father, Kurt Senior, an Indianapolis architect who had cancer, and whose wife had committed suicide some fifteen years earlier, was arrested for running a red light in his hometown. It turned out that he hadn't had a driver's license for twenty years!

You know what he told the arresting officer? "So shoot me," he said.

The African-American jazz pianist Fats Waller had a sentence he used to shout when his playing was absolutely brilliant and hilarious. This was it: "Somebody shoot me while I'm happy!"

That there are such devices as firearms, as easy to operate as cigarette lighters and as cheap as toasters, capable at anybody's whim of killing Father or Fats or Abraham Lincoln or John Lennon or Martin Luther King, Jr., or a woman pushing a baby carriage, should be proof enough for anybody that, to quote the old science fiction writer Kilgore Trout, "being alive is a crock of shit."

2

Imagine this: A great American university gives up football in the name of sanity. It turns its vacant stadium into a bomb factory. So much for sanity. Shades of Kilgore Trout.

I am speaking of my alma mater, the University of Chicago. In December of 1942, long before I got there, the first chain reaction of uranium on Earth was compelled by scientists underneath the stands of Stagg Field. Their intent was to demonstrate the feasibility of an atomic bomb. We were at war with Germany and Japan.

Fifty-three years later, on August 6th, 1995, there was a gathering in the chapel of my university to commemorate the fiftieth anniversary of the detonation of the first atomic bomb, over the city of Hiroshima, Japan. I was there.

One of the speakers was the physicist Leo Seren. He had participated in the successful experiment under the lifeless sports facility so long ago. Get this: He *apologized* for having done that!

Somebody should have told him that being a physicist, on a planet where the smartest animals hate being alive so much, means never having to say you're sorry.

Now imagine this: A man creates a hydrogen bomb for a paranoid Soviet Union, makes sure it will work, and then wins a Nobel Peace Prize! This real-life character, worthy of a story by Kilgore Trout, was the late physicist Andrei Sakharov.

He won his Nobel in 1975 for demanding a halt to the testing of nuclear weapons. He, of course, had already tested *his*. His wife was a pediatrician! What sort of person could perfect a hydrogen bomb while married to a child-care specialist? What sort of physician would stay with a mate that cracked?

"Anything interesting happen at work today, Honeybunch?"

"Yes. My bomb is going to work just great. And how are you doing with that kid with chicken pox?"

Andrei Sakharov was a sort of saint in 1975, a sort that is no longer celebrated, now that the Cold War is over. He was a *dissident* in the Soviet Union. He called for an end to the development and testing of nuclear weapons, and also for more freedoms for his people. He was kicked out of the USSR's Academy of Sciences. He was exiled from Moscow to a whistlestop on the permafrost.

He was not allowed to go to Oslo to receive his Peace Prize. His pediatrician wife, Elena Bonner, accepted it for him there. But isn't it time for us to ask now if she, or any pediatrician or healer, wasn't more deserving of a Peace Prize than anyone who had a hand in creating an H-bomb for any kind of government anywhere?

Human rights? What could be more indifferent to the rights of any form of life than an H-bomb?

. . . . .

Sakharov was in June of 1987 awarded an honorary doctorate by Staten Island College in New York City. Once again his government wouldn't let him accept in person. So I was asked to do that for him.

All I had to do was deliver a message he had sent. This was it: "Don't give up on nuclear energy." I spoke it like a robot.

I was so polite! But this was one year after this crazy planet's most deadly nuclear calamity so far, at Chernobyl, Ukraine. Children all over northern Europe will be sickened or worse for years to come by that release of radiation. Plenty of work for pediatricians!

More heartening to me than Sakharov's cockamamie exhortation was the behavior of firemen in Schenectady, New York, after Chernobyl. I used to work in Schenectady. The firemen sent a letter to their brother firemen over there, congratulating them on their courage and selflessness while trying to save lives and property.

Hooray for firemen!

Scum of the Earth as some may be in their daily lives, they can all be saints in emergencies.

Hooray for firemen.

3

In *Timequake One,* Kilgore Trout wrote a story about an atom bomb. Because of the timequake, he had to write it twice. The ten-year rerun following the timequake, remember, made him and me, *and you,* and everybody else, do everything we'd done from February 17th, 1991, to February 13th, 2001, a second time.

Trout didn't mind writing it again. Rerun or not, he could tune out the crock of shit being alive was as long as he was scribbling, head down, with a ballpoint pen on a yellow legal pad.

He called the story "No Laughing Matter." He threw it away before anybody else could see it, and then had to throw it away again during the rerun. At the clambake at the end of *Timequake One,* in the summer of the year 2001, after free will kicked in again, Trout said this about all the stories he had torn to pieces and flushed down toilets, or tossed into trash-strewn vacant lots, or whatever: "Easy come, easy go."

"No Laughing Matter" got its title from what a judge in the story said during a top-secret court-martial of the crew of the American bomber *Joy's Pride,* on the Pacific island of Banalulu, one month after the end of World War Two.

Joy's Pride itself was perfectly OK, and in a hangar there on Banalulu. It was named in honor of the pilot's mother, Joy Peterson, a nurse in obstetrics in a hospital in Corpus Christi, Texas. *Pride* had a double meaning. It meant self-respect. It meant a lion family, too.

Here's the thing: After an atom bomb was dropped on Hiroshima, and then another one was dropped on Nagasaki, *Joy's Pride* was ordered to drop yet another one on Yokohama, on a couple of million "little yellow bastards." The little yellow bastards were called "little yellow bastards" back then. It was wartime. Trout described the third atom bomb like this: "A purple motherfucker as big as a boiler in the basement of a mid-size junior high school."

It was too big to fit inside the bomb bay. It was slung underneath the plane's belly, and cleared the runway by a foot when *Joy's Pride* took off into the wild blue yonder.

As the plane neared its target, the pilot mused out loud on the intercom that his mother, the obstetrics nurse, would be a celebrity back home after they did what they were about to do. The bomber *Enola Gay,* and the woman in whose honor it was named, had become as famous as movie stars after it dropped its load on Hiroshima. Yokohama was twice as populous as Hiroshima and Nagasaki combined.

The more the pilot thought about it, though, the surer he was that his sweet widowed mother could never tell reporters she was happy that her son's airplane had killed a world's record number of civilians all at once.

· · · · ·

Trout's story reminds me of the time my late great-aunt Emma Vonnegut said she hated the Chinese. Her late son-in-law Kerfuit Stewart, who used to own Stewart's Book Store in Louisville, Kentucky, admonished her that it was *wicked* to hate that many people all at once.

Whatever.

The crewmen aboard *Joy's Pride,* at any rate, told the pilot on the intercom that they felt much as he did. They were all alone up there in the sky. They didn't need a fighter escort, since the Japanese didn't have any airlanes left. The war was over, except for the paperwork, arguably the situation even before *Enola Gay* cremated Hiroshima.

To quote Kilgore Trout: "This wasn't war anymore, and neither had been the obliteration of Nagasaki. This was 'Thanks to the Yanks for a job well done!' This was *show biz* now."

Trout said in "No Laughing Matter" that the pilot and his bombardier had felt somewhat godlike on previous missions, when they had had nothing more than incendiaries and conventional high explosives to drop on people. "But that was godlike with a little *g*," he wrote. "They identified themselves with minor deities who only avenged and destroyed. Up there in the sky all alone, with the purple motherfucker slung underneath their plane, they felt like the Boss God Himself, who had an option which hadn't been theirs before, which was to be *merciful*."

Trout himself had been in World War Two, but not as an airman and not in the Pacific. He had been a forward observer for the Army field artillery in Europe, a lieutenant with binoculars and a radio, up with the infantry or even ahead of it. He would tell batteries to the rear where their shrapnel or white phosphorus or whatever might help a lot.

He himself had certainly not been merciful, nor, by his own account, had he ever felt he should have been. I asked him at the clambake in 2001, at the writers' retreat Xanadu, what he'd done during the war, which he called "civilization's second unsuccessful attempt to commit suicide."

He said without a scintilla of regret, "I made sandwiches of German soldiers between an erupting Earth and an exploding sky, and in a blizzard of razor blades."

The pilot of *Joy's Pride* made a U-turn way up in the sky. The purple motherfucker was still slung underneath. The pilot headed back for Banalulu. "He did it," wrote Trout, "because that is what his mother would have wanted him to do."

At the top-secret court-martial afterward, everybody was convulsed with laughter at one point in the proceedings. This caused the chief judge to bang his gavel and declare that what those on trial had done was "no laughing matter." What people found so funny was the prosecutor's description of what people did at the base when *Joy's Pride* came in for a landing with the purple motherfucker only a foot above the tarmac. People jumped out of windows. They peed in their pants.

"There were all kinds of collisions between different kinds of vehicles," wrote Kilgore Trout.

No sooner had the judge restored order, though, than a huge crack opened in the floor of the Pacific Ocean. It swallowed Banalulu, court-martial, *Joy's Pride*, unused atom bomb and all.

4

When the excellent German novelist and graphic artist Günter Grass heard that I was born in 1922, he said to me, "There are no males in Europe your age for you to talk to." He himself was a kid during Kilgore Trout's and my war, as were Elie Wiesel and Jerzy Kosinski and Milos Forman, and on and on. I was lucky to be born over here instead of over there, and white and middle-class, and into a house full of books and pictures, and into a large extended family, which exists no more.

I heard the poet Robert Pinsky give a reading this summer, in which he apologized didactically for having had a much nicer life than normal. I should do that, too.

At least I seized the opportunity this past May to thank my birthplace, as a graduation speaker at Butler University. I said, "If I had it to do all over, I would choose to be born again in a hospital in Indianapolis. I would choose to spend my childhood again at 4365 North Illinois

Street, about ten blocks from here, and to again be a product of that city's public schools.

"I would again take courses in bacteriology and qualitative analysis in the summer school of Butler University.

"It was all here for me, just as it has all been for you, the best and the worst of Western Civilization, if you cared to pay attention: music, finance, government, architecture, law and sculpture and painting, history and medicine and athletics and every sort of science, and books, books, books, and teachers and role models.

"People so smart you can't believe it, and people so dumb you can't believe it. People so nice you can't believe it, and people so mean you can't believe it."

I gave advice, too. I said, "My uncle Alex Vonnegut, a Harvard-educated life insurance salesman who lived at 5033 North Pennsylvania Street, taught me something very important. He said that when things were really going well we should be sure to *notice* it.

"He was talking about simple occasions, not great victories: maybe drinking lemonade on a hot afternoon in the shade, or smelling the aroma of a nearby bakery, or fishing and not caring if we catch anything or not, or hearing somebody all alone playing a piano really well in the house next door.

"Uncle Alex urged me to say this out loud during such epiphanies: 'If this isn't nice, what is?' "

Another way I was lucky: for the first thirty-three years of my life, telling short stories with ink on paper was a major American industry. Although I then had a wife and two children, it made good business sense for me to quit my job as a publicity man for General Electric, with health insurance and a retirement plan. I could make more money selling stories to *The Saturday Evening Post* and *Collier's,* weekly magazines full of ads, which published five short stories and an installment of a cliff-hanging serial in every issue.

Those were just the top-paying buyers of what I could produce. There were so many other magazines hungry for fiction that the market for stories was like a pinball machine. When I mailed off a story to my agent, I could be pretty sure somebody would pay me something for it, even though it might be rejected again and again.

But not long after I moved my family from Schenectady, New York, to Cape Cod, television, a much better buy for advertisers than magazines, made playing short story pinball for a living obsolete.

I commuted from the Cape to Boston to work for an industrial advertising agency, and then became a dealer in Saab automobiles, and then taught high school English in a private school for seriously fucked-up rich kids.

My son the doctor Mark Vonnegut, who wrote a swell book about his going crazy in the 1960s, and then graduated from Harvard Medical School, had an exhibition of his watercolors in Milton, Massachusetts, this summer. A reporter asked him what it had been like to grow up with a famous father.

Mark replied, "When I was growing up, my father was a car salesman who couldn't get a job teaching at Cape Cod Junior College."

5

I still think up short stories from time to time, as though there were money in it. The habit dies hard. There used to be fleeting fame in it, too. Highly literate people once talked enthusiastically to one another about a story by Ray Bradbury or J. D. Salinger or John Cheever or John Collier or John O'Hara or Shirley Jackson or Flannery O'Connor or whomever, which had appeared in a magazine in the past few days.

No more.

All I do with short story ideas now is rough them out, credit them to Kilgore Trout, and put them in a novel. Here's the start of another one hacked from the carcass of *Timequake One,* and entitled "The Sisters B-36": "On the matriarchal planet Booboo in the Crab Nebula, there were three sisters whose last name was B-36. It could be only a coincidence that their family name was also that of an Earthling airplane designed to drop bombs on civilian populations with corrupt leaderships. Earth and Booboo were too far apart to ever communicate."

Another coincidence: The written language of Booboo was like

English on Earth, in that it consisted of idiosyncratic arrangements in horizontal lines of twenty-six phonetic symbols, ten numbers, and about eight punctuation marks.

All three of the sisters were beautiful, so went Trout's tale, but only two of them were popular, one a picture painter and the other a short story writer. Nobody could stand the third one, who was a scientist. She was so *boring*! All she could talk about was thermodynamics. She was envious. Her secret ambition was to make her two artistic sisters feel, to use a favorite expression of Trout's, "like something the cat drug in."

Trout said Booboolings were among the most adaptable creatures in the local family of galaxies. This was thanks to their great big brains, which could be programmed to do or not do, and feel or not feel, just about anything. You name it!

The programming wasn't done surgically or electrically, or by any other sort of neurological intrusiveness. It was done *socially*, with nothing but talk, talk, talk. Grownups would speak to little Booboolings favorably about presumably appropriate and desirable feelings and deeds. The brains of the youngsters would respond by growing circuits that made civilized pleasures and behavior automatic.

It seemed a good idea, for example, when nothing much was really going on, for Booboolings to be beneficially excited by minimal stimuli, such as idiosyncratic arrangements in horizontal lines of twenty-six phonetic symbols, ten numbers, and eight or so punctuation marks, or dabs of pigment on flat surfaces in frames.

When a little Boobooling was reading a book, a grownup might interrupt to say, depending on what was happening in the book, "Isn't that sad? The little girl's nice little dog has just been run over by a garbage truck. Doesn't that make you want to cry?" Or the grownup might say, about a very different sort of story, "Isn't that funny? When that conceited old rich man stepped on a *nim-nim* peel and fell into an open manhole, didn't that make you practically pop a gut laughing?"

A *nim-nim* was a banana-like fruit on Booboo.

An immature Boobooling taken to an art gallery might be asked about a certain painting whether the woman in it was really smiling or not. Couldn't she be sad about something, and still look that way? Is she married, do you think? Does she have a kid? Is she nice to it? Where do you think she's going next? Does she want to go?

If there was a bowl of fruit in the painting, a grownup might ask, "Don't those *nim-nims* look good enough to eat? Yummy yum yum!"

These examples of Boobooling pedagogy aren't mine. They're Kilgore Trout's.

Thus were the brains of most, but not quite all, Booboolings made to grow circuits, microchips, if you like, which on Earth would be called *imaginations.* Yes, and it was precisely because a vast majority of Booboolings had imaginations that two of the B-36 sisters, the short story writer and the painter, were so beloved.

The bad sister had an imagination, all right, but not in the field of art appreciation. She wouldn't read books or go to art galleries. She spent every spare minute when she was little in the garden of a lunatic asylum next door. The psychos in the garden were believed to be harmless, so her keeping them company was regarded as a laudably compassionate activity. But the nuts taught her thermodynamics and calculus and so on.

When the bad sister was a young woman, she and the nuts worked up designs for television cameras and transmitters and receivers. Then she got money from her very rich mom to manufacture and market these satanic devices, which made imaginations redundant. They were instantly popular because the shows were so attractive and no thinking was involved.

She made a lot of money, but what really pleased her was that her two sisters were starting to feel like something the cat drug in. Young Booboolings didn't see any point in developing imaginations anymore, since all they had to do was turn on a switch and see all kinds of jazzy shit. They would look at a printed page or a painting and wonder how anybody could have gotten his or her rocks off looking at things that simple and dead.

The bad sister's name was Nim-nim. When her parents named her that, they had no idea how unsweet she was going to be. And TV wasn't the half of it! She was as unpopular as ever because she was as boring as ever, so she invented automobiles and computers and barbed wire and flamethrowers and land mines and machine guns and so on. That's how pissed off she was.

New generations of Booboolings grew up without imaginations. Their appetites for diversions from boredom were perfectly satisfied by all the crap Nim-nim was selling them. Why not? What the heck.

Without imaginations, though, they couldn't do what their ancestors had done, which was read interesting, heartwarming stories in the faces of one another. So, according to Kilgore Trout, "Booboolings became among the most merciless creatures in the local family of galaxies."

6

Trout said at the clambake in 2001 that life was undeniably preposterous. "But our brains are big enough to let us adapt to the inevitable pratfalls and buffoonery," he went on, "by means of manmade epiphanies like this one." He meant the clambake on a beach under a starry sky. "If this isn't nice, what is?" he said.

He declared the corn on the cob, steamed in seaweed with lobsters and clams, to be *heavenly*. He added, "And don't all the ladies look like *angels* tonight!" He was feasting on corn on the cob and women as *ideas*. He couldn't eat the corn because the upper plate of his false teeth was insecure. His long-term relationships with women had been disasters. In the only love story he ever attempted, "Kiss Me Again," he had written, "There is no way a beautiful woman can live up to what she looks like for any appreciable length of time."

The moral at the end of that story is this: "Men are jerks. Women are psychotic."

. . . . .

Chief among manmade epiphanies for me have been stage plays. Trout called them "artificial timequakes." He said, "Before Earthlings knew there were such things as timequakes in Nature, they invented them." And it's true. Actors know everything they are going to say and do, and how everything is going to come out in the end, for good or ill, when the curtain goes up on Act One, Scene One. Yet they have no choice but to behave as though the future were a mystery.

Yes, and when the timequake of 2001 zapped us back to 1991, it made ten years of our pasts ten years of our futures, so we could remember everything we had to say and do again when the time came.

Keep this in mind at the start of the next rerun after the next timequake: *The show must go on!*

The artificial timequake that has moved me most so far this year is an old one. It is *Our Town*, by the late Thornton Wilder. I had already watched it with undiminished satisfaction maybe five or six times. And then this spring my thirteen-year-old daughter, dear Lily, was cast as a talking dead person in the graveyard of Grover's Corners in a school production of that innocent, sentimental masterpiece.

The play zapped Lily and her schoolmates from the evening of the performance back to May 7th, 1901! Timequake! They were robots of Thornton Wilder's imaginary past until the curtain came down after the funeral of the heroine Emily in the very last scene. Only then could they live in 1996 again. Only then could they again decide for themselves what to say or do next. Only then could they exercise free will again.

I reflected sadly that night, with Lily pretending to be a dead grownup, that I would be seventy-eight when she graduated from high school, and eighty-two when she graduated from college, and so on. Talk about remembering the future!

What hit me really hard that night, though, was the character Emily's farewell in the last scene, after the mourners have gone back down the hill to their village, having buried her. She says, "Good-by, good-by, world. Good-by, Grover's Corners . . . Mama and Papa. Good-by to clocks ticking . . . and Mama's sunflowers. And food and coffee. And new-ironed dresses and hot baths . . . and sleeping and waking up. Oh, earth, you're too wonderful for anybody to realize you.

"Do any human beings ever realize life while they live it?—every, every minute?"

I myself become a sort of Emily every time I hear that speech. I haven't died yet, but there is a place, as seemingly safe and simple, as learnable, as acceptable as Grover's Corners at the turn of the century, with ticking clocks and Mama and Papa and hot baths and new-ironed clothes and all the rest of it, to which I've already said good-by, good-by, one hell of a long time ago now.

Here's what that was: the first seven years of my life, before the shit hit the fan, first the Great Depression and then World War Two.

They say the first thing to go when you're old is your legs or your eyesight. It isn't true. The first thing to go is parallel parking.

Now I find myself maundering about parts of plays hardly anybody knows or cares about anymore, such as the graveyard scene in *Our Town*, or the poker game in Tennessee Williams's *A Streetcar Named Desire*, or what Willy Loman's wife said after that tragically ordinary, clumsily gallant American committed suicide in Arthur Miller's *Death of a Salesman*.

She said, "Attention must be paid."

In *A Streetcar Named Desire,* Blanche DuBois said as she was taken away to a madhouse, after she was raped by her sister's husband, "I have always depended on the kindness of strangers."

Those speeches, those situations, those people, became emotional and ethical landmarks for me in my early manhood, and remain such in the summer of 1996. That is because I was immobilized in a congregation of rapt fellow human beings in a theater when I first saw and heard them.

They would have made no more impression on me than *Monday Night Football,* had I been alone eating nachos and gazing into the face of a cathode-ray tube.

In the early days of television, when there were only half a dozen channels at most, significant, well-written dramas on a cathode-ray tube could still make us feel like members of an attentive congregation, alone at home as we might be. There was a high probability back then, with so few shows to choose from, that friends and neighbors were watching the same show we were watching, still finding TV a whizbang miracle.

We might even call up a friend that very night, and ask a question to which we already knew the answer: "Did you see *that?* Wow!"

No more.

7

I wouldn't have missed the Great Depression or my part in World War Two for anything. Trout asserted at the clambake that our war would live forever in show biz, as other wars would not, because of the uniforms of the Nazis.

He commented unfavorably on the camouflage suits our own generals wear nowadays on TV, when they describe our blasting the bejesus out of some Third World country because of petroleum. "I can't imagine," he said, "any part of the world where such garish pajamas would make a soldier less rather than more visible.

"We are evidently preparing," he said, "to fight World War Three in the midst of an enormous Spanish omelet."

He asked what relatives of mine had been wounded in wars. As far as I knew, only one. That was my great-grandfather Peter Lieber, an immigrant who became a brewer in Indianapolis after being wounded in one leg during our Civil War. He was a Freethinker, which is to say a skeptic about conventional religious beliefs, as had been Voltaire and

Thomas Jefferson and Benjamin Franklin and so on. And as would be Kilgore Trout and I.

I told Trout that Peter Lieber's Anglo-American company commander gave his men, all Freethinkers from Germany, Christian religious tracts for inspiration. Trout responded by giving his own revision of the Book of Genesis.

Fortunately, I had a tape recorder, which I turned on.

"Please stop eating and pay attention," he said. "This is important." He paused to press the upper plate of his false teeth against the roof of his mouth with the ball of his left thumb. It would come unstuck again every two minutes or so. He was left-handed, as was I until my parents made me switch, and as are my daughters Edith and Lily, or, as we call them affectionately, Edie Bucket and Lolly-boo.

"In the beginning there was absolutely nothing, and I mean *nothing*," he said. "But nothing implies something, just as up implies down and sweet implies sour, as man implies woman and drunk implies sober and happy implies sad. I hate to tell you this, friends and neighbors, but we are teensy-weensy implications in an enormous implication. If you don't like it here, why don't you go back to where you came from?"

"The first something to be implied by all the nothing," he said, "was in fact two somethings, who were God and Satan. God was male. Satan was female. They implied each other, and hence were peers in the emerging power structure, which was itself nothing but an implication. Power was implied by weakness."

"God created the heaven and the earth," the old, long-out-of-print science fiction writer went on. "And the earth was without form, and void, and darkness was upon the face of the deep. And the spirit of God moved upon the face of the waters. Satan could have done this herself, but she thought it was stupid, action for the sake of action. What was the point? She didn't say anything at first.

"But Satan began to worry about God when He said, 'Let there be light,' and there was light. She had to wonder, 'What in heck does He think He's doing? How far does He intend to go, and does He expect me to help Him take care of all this crazy stuff?'

"And then the shit really hit the fan. God made man and woman, beautiful little miniatures of Him and her, and turned them loose to see what might become of them. The Garden of Eden," said Trout, "might be considered the prototype for the Colosseum and the Roman Games."

"Satan," he said, "couldn't undo anything God had done. She could at least try to make existence for His little toys less painful. She could see what He couldn't: To be alive was to be either bored or scared stiff. So she filled an apple with all sorts of ideas that might at least relieve the boredom, such as rules for games with cards and dice, and how to fuck, and recipes for beer and wine and whiskey, and pictures of different plants that were smokable, and so on. And instructions on how to make music and sing and dance real crazy, real sexy. And how to spout blasphemy when they stubbed their toes.

"Satan had a serpent give Eve the apple. Eve took a bite and handed it to Adam. He took a bite, and then they fucked."

"I grant you," said Trout, "that some of the ideas in the apple had catastrophic side effects for a minority of those who tried them." Let it

25

be noted here that Trout himself was not an alcoholic, a junkie, a gambler, or a sex fiend. He just wrote.

"All Satan wanted to do was help, and she did in many cases," he concluded. "And her record for promoting nostrums with occasionally dreadful side effects is no worse than that of the most reputable pharmaceutical houses of the present day."

8

Side effects of Satan's booze recipes have played a deleterious part in the lives and deaths of many great American writers. In *Timequake One,* I envisioned a writers' retreat called Xanadu, where each of the four guest suites was named in honor of an American winner of a Nobel Prize for Literature. The Ernest Hemingway and Eugene O'Neill were on the second floor of the mansion. The Sinclair Lewis was on the third. The John Steinbeck was in the carriage house.

Kilgore Trout exclaimed upon arriving at Xanadu, two weeks after free will kicked in again, "All four of your ink-on-paper heroes were certifiable alcoholics!"

Gambling ruined William Saroyan. A combination of booze and gambling did in the journalist Alvin Davis, a much-missed friend of mine. I asked Al one time what was the biggest kick he got from games of chance. He said it came after he had lost all his money in an around-the-clock poker game.

He went back after a few hours with money he had gotten wherever he could get it, from a friend, from hocking something, from a loan-shark. And he sat down at the table and said, "Deal me in."

. . . . .

The late British philosopher Bertrand Russell said he lost friends to one of three addictions: alcohol or religion or chess. Kilgore Trout was hooked on making idiosyncratic arrangements in horizontal lines, with ink on bleached and flattened wood pulp, of twenty-six phonetic symbols, ten numbers, and about eight punctuation marks. He was a black hole to anyone who might imagine that he or she was a friend of his.

I have been married twice, divorced once. Both my wives, Jane and now Jill, have said on occasion that I am much like Trout in that regard.

My mother was addicted to being rich, to servants and unlimited charge accounts, to giving lavish dinner parties, to taking frequent first-class trips to Europe. So one might say she was tormented by withdrawal symptoms all through the Great Depression.

She was *acculturated*!

Acculturated persons are those who find that they are no longer treated as the sort of people they thought they were, because the outside world has changed. An economic misfortune or a new technology, or being conquered by another country or political faction, can do that to people quicker than you can say "Jack Robinson."

As Trout wrote in his "An American Family Marooned on the Planet Pluto": "Nothing wrecks any kind of love more effectively than the discovery that your previously acceptable behavior has become ridiculous." He said in conversation at the 2001 clambake: "If I hadn't learned how to live without a culture and a society, acculturation would have broken my heart a thousand times."

. . . . .

In *Timequake One,* I had Trout discard his "The Sisters B-36" in a lidless wire trash receptacle chained to a fire hydrant in front of the American Academy of Arts and Letters, way-the-hell-and-gone up on West 155th Street in Manhattan, two doors west of Broadway. This was on the afternoon of Christmas Eve, 2000, supposedly fifty-one days before the timequake zapped everybody and everything back to 1991.

The members of the Academy, I said, who were addicted to making old-fashioned art in old-fashioned ways, without computers, were experiencing acculturation. They were like the two artistic sisters on the matriarchal planet Booboo in the Crab Nebula.

There really is an American Academy of Arts and Letters. Its palatial headquarters are where I placed them in *Timequake One.* There really is a fire hydrant out front. There really is a library inside, and an art gallery and reception halls and meeting rooms and staff offices, and a very grand auditorium.

By an act of Congress passed in 1916, the Academy can have no more than 250 members, American citizens, all of whom have distinguished themselves as novelists, dramatists, poets, historians, essayists, critics, composers of music, architects, painters, or sculptors. Their ranks are regularly diminished by the Grim Reaper, by death. A task of the survivors is to nominate and then, by secret ballot, elect persons to fill the vacancies.

Among the Academy's founders were old-fashioned writers such as Henry Adams and William and Henry James, and Samuel Clemens, and the old-fashioned composer Edward MacDowell. Their audiences were necessarily small. Their own brains were all they had to work with.

I said in *Timequake One* that by the year 2000, craftspeople of their sort had become "as quaint," in the opinion of the general public, "as contemporary makers in New England tourist towns of the toy windmills known since colonial times as *whirligigs*."

9

Founders of the Academy at the turn of the century were contemporaneous with Thomas Alva Edison, inventor of, among other things, sound recordings and motion pictures. Before World War Two, though, these schemes for holding the attention of millions all over the world were only squawking or flickering lampoons of life itself.

The Academy occupied its present home, designed by the firm of McKim, Mead & White, and paid for by the philanthropist Archer Milton Huntington, in 1923. In that year, the American inventor Lee De Forest demonstrated apparatus that made possible the addition of sound to motion pictures.

I had a scene in *Timequake One*, set in the office of Monica Pepper, fictitious Executive Secretary of the Academy, on Christmas Eve, 2000. That was the afternoon on which Kilgore Trout put "The Sisters B-36" in the lidless wire trash receptacle out front, again, fifty-one days before the timequake struck.

Mrs. Pepper, wife of the wheelchair-ridden composer Zoltan Pepper, bore a striking resemblance to my late sister Allie, who hated life so much. Allie died of cancer of the everything way back in 1958, when I was thirty-six and she was forty-one, hounded by bill collectors to the very end. Both women were pretty blondes, which was OK. But they were six-foot-two! Both women were permanently acculturated in adolescence, since nowhere on Earth, save among the Watusis, did it make any sense for a woman to be that tall.

Both women were unlucky. Allie married a nice guy who lost all their money and then some in dumb businesses. Monica Pepper was the reason her husband Zoltan was paralyzed from the waist down. Two years earlier, she had accidentally landed on top of him in a swimming pool out in Aspen, Colorado. At least Allie had to die so deep in debt, and with four sons to raise, only once. After the timequake struck, Monica Pepper would have to swan-dive on top of her husband a second time.

Monica and Zoltan were talking in her office at the Academy that Christmas Eve, 2000. Zoltan was crying and laughing simultaneously. They were the same age, forty, which made them baby boomers. They didn't have any kids. Because of her, his ding-dong didn't work anymore. Zoltan was crying and laughing about that, certainly, but mostly about a tone-deaf kid next door, who had composed and orchestrated an acceptable, if derivative, string quartet in the manner of Beethoven, with the help of a new computer program called Wolfgang.

Nothing would do but that the father of the obnoxious kid show Zoltan the sheet music his son's printer had spit out that morning and ask him if it was any good or not.

As though Zoltan weren't sufficiently destabilized emotionally by legs and a ding-dong that didn't work anymore, his older brother Frank, an architect, had committed suicide after a nearly identical blow to his self-respect only a month earlier. Yes, and Frank Pepper would eventually be popped out of his grave by the timequake, so he could blow his brains out while his wife and three kids watched a second time.

Here's the thing: Frank went to the drugstore for condoms or chewing gum or whatever, and the pharmacist told him that his sixteen-year-old daughter had become an architect and was thinking of dropping out of high school because it was such a waste of time. She had designed a recreation center for teenagers in depressed neighborhoods with the help of a new computer program the school had bought for its vocational students, dummies who weren't going to anything but junior colleges. It was called Palladio.

Frank went to a computer store, and asked if he could try out Palladio before buying it. He doubted very much that it could help anyone with his native talent and education. So right there in the store, and in a period of no more than half an hour, Palladio gave him what he had asked it for, working drawings that would enable a contractor to build a three-story parking garage in the manner of Thomas Jefferson.

Frank had made up the craziest assignment he could think of, confident that Palladio would tell him to take his custom elsewhere. But it didn't! It presented him with menu after menu, asking how many cars, and in what city, because of various local building codes, and whether trucks would be allowed to use it, too, and on and on. It even asked about surrounding buildings, and whether Jeffersonian architecture would be in harmony with them. It offered to give him alternative plans in the manner of Michael Graves or I. M. Pei.

It gave him plans for the wiring and plumbing, and ballpark estimates of what it would cost to build in any part of the world he cared to name.

So Frank went home and killed himself the first time.

· · · · ·

Laughing and crying there in his wife's office at the Academy on the first of two Christmas Eves, 2000, Zoltan Pepper said this to his pretty but gawky wife: "It used to be said of a man who had suffered a catastrophic setback in his line of work that he had been handed his head on a platter. We are being handed our heads with *tweezers* now."

He was speaking, of course, of microchips.

10

Allie died in New Jersey. She and her husband, Jim, also a native Hoosier, are buried whole in Crown Hill Cemetery in Indianapolis. So is James Whitcomb Riley, the *Hoosier Poet*, a never-married lush. So is John Dillinger, the beloved bank robber of the 1930s. So are our parents, Kurt and Edith, and Father's kid brother Alex Vonnegut, the Harvard-educated life insurance salesman who said, whenever life was good, "If this isn't nice, what is?" So are two previous generations of our parents' forebears: a brewer, an architect, merchants and musicians, and their wives, of course.

Full house!

John Dillinger, a farm boy, escaped from jail once brandishing a wooden pistol he had whittled from a broken washtub slat. He blackened it with shoe polish! He was so *entertaining*. While on the run, robbing banks and vanishing into the boondocks, Dillinger wrote Henry Ford a fan letter. He thanked the old anti-Semite for making such fast and agile getaway cars!

It was possible to get away from the police back then if you were a better driver with a better car. Talk about *fair play*! Talk about what we say we want for everyone in America: *a level playing field!* And Dillinger robbed only the rich and strong, banks with armed guards, and *in person*.

Dillinger wasn't a simpering, sly swindler. He was an *athlete*.

In the slavering search for subversive literature on the shelves of our public schools, which will never stop, the two most subversive tales of all remain untouched, wholly unsuspected. One is the story of Robin Hood. As ill educated as John Dillinger was, that was surely his inspiration: a *reputable* blueprint for what a real man might *do* with life.

The minds of children in intellectually humble American homes back then weren't swamped with countless stories from TV sets. They heard or read only a few stories, and so could remember them, and maybe learn something from them. Everywhere in the English-speaking world, one of those was "Cinderella." Another was "The Ugly Duckling." Another was the story of Robin Hood.

And another, as disrespectful of established authority as the story of Robin Hood, which "Cinderella" and "The Ugly Duckling" are not, is the life of Jesus Christ as described in the New Testament.

G-men, under orders from J. Edgar Hoover, the unmarried homosexual director of the FBI, shot Dillinger dead, simply executed him as he came out of a movie theater with a date. He hadn't pulled a gun, or lunged or dived, or tried to run away. He was like anybody else coming out into the real world after a movie, awakening from enchantment. He was killed because he had for too long made G-men, all of whom then wore fedoras, look non compos mentis, like nincompoops.

That was in 1934. I was eleven. Allie was sixteen. Allie wept and raged, and we both reviled Dillinger's date at the movie. This *bitch*, and there was nothing else to call her, tipped off the feds about where Dillinger would be that night. She said she would be wearing an orange dress. The nondescript gink by her side when she came out would be the man the gay director of the FBI had branded Public Enemy Number One.

She was Hungarian. As the old saying goes: "If you have a Hungarian for a friend, you don't need an enemy."

Allie later had her picture taken with Dillinger's big tombstone at Crown Hill, not far from the fence on West Thirty-eighth Street. I myself came upon it from time to time, while shooting crows with a .22 semiautomatic rifle our gun-nut father gave me for my birthday. Crows back then were classified as enemies of mankind. Given half a chance, they would eat our corn.

One kid I knew shot a golden eagle. You should have seen the wingspread!

Allie hated hunting so much that I stopped doing it, and so did Father. As I've written elsewhere, he had become a gun nut and hunter in order to prove that he wasn't effeminate, even though he was in the arts, an architect and a painter and potter. In public lectures, I myself often say, "If you really want to hurt your parents, and you don't have nerve enough to be a homosexual, the least you can do is go into the arts."

Father supposed he could still demonstrate his manhood by fishing. But then my big brother Bernie spoiled that for him, too, saying it was as though he were smashing up Swiss pocketwatches, or some other exquisitely engineered little pieces of machinery.

· · · · ·

I told Kilgore Trout at the clambake in 2001 about how my brother and sister had made Father ashamed of hunting and fishing. He quoted Shakespeare: "How sharper than a serpent's tooth it is to have a thankless child!"

Trout was self-educated, never having finished high school. I was mildly surprised, then, that he could quote Shakespeare. I asked if he had committed a lot of that remarkable author's words to memory. He said, "Yes, dear colleague, including a single sentence which describes life as lived by human beings so completely that no writer after him need ever have written another word."

"Which sentence was that, Mr. Trout?" I asked.

And he said, " 'All the world's a stage, and all the men and women merely players.' "

11

I wrote a letter to an old friend last spring about why I evidently couldn't write publishable fiction anymore, after trying and failing to do that for many years. He is Edward Muir, a poet and advertising man my age living in Scarsdale. In my novel *Cat's Cradle*, I say that anybody whose life keeps tangling up with yours for no logical reason is likely a member of your *karass*, a team God has formed to get something done for Him. Ed Muir is surely a member of my *karass*.

Listen to this: When I was at the University of Chicago after World War Two, Ed was there, although we did not meet. When I went to Schenectady, New York, to be a publicist for the General Electric Company, Ed went there to be a teacher at Union College. When I quit GE and moved to Cape Cod, he showed up there as a recruiter for the Great Books Program. At last we met, and whether in the service of God or not, my first wife Jane and I became leaders of a Great Books group.

And when he took an advertising job in Boston, so did I, not knowing he had done that. When Ed's first marriage broke up, so did mine, and now we're both in New York. My point, though, is as follows: When I sent him a letter about my case of writer's block, he made it look like a poem and returned it.

He left off my salutation and the first few lines, which were in praise of *Reader's Block* by David Markson, who had been his student at Union College. I said David shouldn't thank Fate for letting him write such a good book in a time when large numbers of people could no longer be wowed by a novel, no matter how excellent. Something like that. I don't have a copy of my letter as prose. As a poem, though, this is its appearance:

And no thanks to Fate.
When we're gone, there won't be anybody
Sufficiently excited by ink on paper
To realize how good it is.

I have this ailment not unlike
Ambulatory pneumonia, which might be called
Ambulatory writer's block.

I cover paper with words every day,
But the stories never go anywhere
I find worth going.

Slaughterhouse-Five *has been turned*
Into an opera by a young German,
And will have its premiere in Munich this June.
I'm not going there either.
Not interested.

I am fond of Occam's Razor,
Or the Law of Parsimony, which suggests
That the simplest explanation of a phenomenon
Is usually the most trustworthy.

And I now believe, with David's help,
That writer's block is finding out
How lives of loved ones really ended
Instead of the way we hoped they would end
With the help of our body English.
Fiction is body English.

Whatever.

It was nice of Ed to do that. Another nice story about him is from his days as a road man for Great Books. He is a minor poet, publishing occasionally in *The Atlantic Monthly* and suchlike. His name, though, is nearly identical with that of the major poet Edwin Muir, a Scotsman who died in 1959. Hazily sophisticated people sometimes asked him if he was *the poet,* meaning Edwin.

One time, when Ed told a woman he wasn't *the poet,* she expressed deep disappointment. She said one of her favorite poems was "The Poet Covers His Child." Get a load of this: It was the American Ed Muir who wrote that poem.

12

I wish I'd written *Our Town*. I wish I'd invented Rollerblades.

I asked A. E. Hotchner, a friend and biographer of the late Ernest Hemingway, if Hemingway had ever shot a human being, not counting himself. Hotchner said, "No."

I asked the late great German novelist Heinrich Böll what the basic flaw was in the German character. He said, "Obedience."

I asked one of my adopted nephews what he thought of my dancing. He said, "Acceptable."

When I took a job in Boston as an advertising copywriter, because I was broke, an account executive asked me what kind of name Vonnegut was. I said, "German." He said, "Germans killed six million of my cousins."

You want to know why I don't have AIDS, why I'm not HIV-positive like so many other people? I don't fuck around. It's as simple as that.

Trout said this was the story on why AIDS and new strains of syph and clap and the blueballs were making the rounds like Avon ladies run amok: On September 1st of 1945, immediately after the end of World War Two, representatives of all the chemical elements held a meeting on the planet Tralfamadore. They were there to protest some of their members' having been incorporated into the bodies of big, sloppy, stinky organisms as cruel and stupid as human beings.

Elements such as Polonium and Ytterbium, which had never been essential parts of human beings, were nonetheless outraged that *any* chemicals should be so misused.

Carbon, although an embarrassed veteran of countless massacres throughout history, focused the attention of the meeting on the public execution of only one man, accused of treason in fifteenth-century England. He was hanged until almost dead. He was revived. His abdomen was slit open.

The executioner pulled out a loop of his intestines. He dangled the loop before the man's face and burned it with a torch here and there. The loop was still attached to the rest of the man's insides. The executioner and his assistants tied a horse to each of his four limbs.

They whipped the horses, which ripped the man into four jagged pieces. These were hung on display from meathooks in a marketplace.

·   ·   ·   ·   ·

It had been agreed before the meeting was called to order that no one was to tell of terrible things grown-up human beings had done to children, according to Trout. Several delegates threatened to boycott the meeting if they were expected to sit still while listening to tales that sickening. What would be the point?

"What grownups had done to grownups left no doubt that the human race should be exterminated," said Trout. "Rehashing ad nauseam what grownups had done to children would be gilding the lily, so to speak."

Nitrogen wept about its involuntary servitude as parts of Nazi guards and physicians in death camps during World War Two. Potassium told hair-raising stories about the Spanish Inquisition, and Calcium about the Roman Games, and Oxygen about black African slavery.

Sodium said enough was enough, that any further testimony would be coals to Newcastle. It made a motion that all chemicals involved in medical research combine whenever possible to create ever more powerful antibiotics. These in turn would cause disease organisms to evolve new strains that were resistant to them.

In no time, Sodium predicted, every human ailment, including acne and jock itch, would be not only incurable but fatal. "All humans will die," said Sodium, according to Trout. "As they were at the birth of the Universe, all elements will be free of sin again."

Iron and Magnesium seconded Sodium's motion. Phosphorus called for a vote. The motion was passed by acclamation.

13

Kilgore Trout was right next door to the American Academy of Arts and Letters on Christmas Eve, 2000, when Zoltan Pepper said to his wife that people were now getting their heads handed to them with tweezers instead of on platters. Trout couldn't hear him. There was a thick masonry wall between them as the paraplegic composer ranted on about the seeming mania for making people compete with machines that were smarter than they were.

Pepper asked this rhetorical question: "Why is it so important that we all be humiliated, with such ingenuity and at such great expense? We never thought we were such hot stuff in the first place."

Trout was sitting on his cot in a shelter for homeless men that was once the Museum of the American Indian. Arguably the most prolific writer of short stories in history, he had been caught by the police in a sweep of the New York Public Library down at Fifth Avenue and Forty-second Street. He and about thirty others who had been living there, what Trout called "sacred cattle," were carted off in a black school bus and deposited in the shelter way-the-hell-and-gone up on West 155th Street.

The Museum of the American Indian had moved the detritus of overwhelmed aborigines, and dioramas of how they lived before the shit hit the fan, into a safer neighborhood downtown, five years before Trout arrived.

He was eighty-four years old now, having passed another milestone on November 11th, 2000. He would die on Labor Day, 2001, still eighty-four. But by then the timequake would have given him and all the rest of us an unexpected *bonus,* if you can call it that, of another ten years.

He would write of the rerun when it was over, in a never-to-be-finished memoir entitled *My Ten Years on Automatic Pilot*: "Listen, if it isn't a timequake dragging us through knothole after knothole, it's something else just as mean and powerful."

"This was a man," I said in *Timequake One,* "an only child, whose father, a college professor in Northampton, Massachusetts, murdered his mother when the man was only twelve years old."

I said Trout had been a hobo, throwing away his stories instead of offering them to publications, since the autumn of 1975. I said that was after he received news of the death of his own only child, Leon, a deserter from the United States Marine Corps. Leon, I said, was accidentally decapitated in a shipyard accident in Sweden, where he had been granted political asylum and was working as a welder.

I said Trout was fifty-nine when he hit the road, never to have a home again until he was given, when he was about to die, the Ernest Hemingway Suite at the Rhode Island writers' retreat called Xanadu.

. . . . .

When Trout checked into the former Museum of the American Indian, a former reminder of the most extensive and persistent genocide known to history, "The Sisters B-36" was burning a hole in his pocket, so to speak. He had finished the story at the Public Library downtown, but the police had taken him into custody before he could get rid of it.

So he kept his war-surplus Navy overcoat on when he told the clerk at the shelter that his name was Vincent van Gogh, and that he had no living relatives. Then he went outdoors again, and it was cold enough to freeze the balls off a brass monkey out there, and he put the manuscript into the lidless wire trash receptacle, which was chained and padlocked to a fire hydrant in front of the American Academy of Arts and Letters.

When he got back into the shelter, after an absence of ten minutes, the clerk said to him, "Where have you been? We all sure missed you, Vince." And he told him where his cot was. It was butted up against the companion wall between the shelter and the Academy.

On the Academy side of the wall, hanging over the rosewood desk of Monica Pepper, was a painting of a bleached cow's skull on a desert floor, by Georgia O'Keeffe. On Trout's side, right over the head of his cot, was a poster telling him never to stick his ding-dong into anything without first putting on a condom.

After the timequake hit, and then the rerun was finally over, and free will had kicked in again, Trout and Monica would get to know each other. Her desk, incidentally, had once belonged to the novelist Henry James. Her chair had once belonged to the composer and conductor Leonard Bernstein.

When Trout realized how close his cot had been to her desk during the fifty-one days before the timequake struck, he would remark as follows: "If I'd had a bazooka, I could have blown a hole in the wall between us. If I hadn't killed one or both of us, I could have asked you, 'What's a nice girl like you doing in a place like that?' "

14

A bum on a cot next to Trout's at the shelter wished him a Merry Christmas. Trout replied, "Ting-a-ling! Ting-a-ling!"

It was only by chance that his reply was appropriate to the holiday, alluding, one might suppose, to the bells of Santa Claus's sleigh on a rooftop. But Trout would have said "Ting-a-ling" to anybody who offered him an empty greeting, such as "How's it goin'?" or "Nice day" or whatever, no matter what the season.

Depending on his body language and tone of voice and social circumstances, he could indeed make it mean "And a merry Christmas to you, too." But it would also mean, like the Hawaiian's *aloha*, "Hello" or "Good-bye." The old science fiction writer could make it mean "Please" or "Thanks" as well, or "Yes" or "No," or "I couldn't agree with you more," or "If your brains were dynamite, there wouldn't be enough to blow your hat off."

I asked him at Xanadu in the summer of 2001 how "Ting-a-ling" had become such a frequent *appoggiatura*, or grace note, in his conversations. He gave me what would later turn out to have been a superficial explanation. "It was something I crowed during the war," he said, "when an artillery barrage I'd called for landed right on target: 'Ting-a-ling! Ting-a-ling!' "

About an hour later, and this was on the afternoon before the clambake, he beckoned me into his suite with a crooked finger. He closed the door behind us. "You really want to know about 'Ting-a-ling'?" he asked me.

I had been satisfied with his first account. Trout was the one who wanted me to hear much more. My innocent question earlier had triggered memories of his ghastly childhood in Northampton. He could exorcise them only by telling what they were.

"My father murdered my mother," said Kilgore Trout, "when I was twelve years old."

"Her body was in our basement," said Trout, "but all I knew was that she had disappeared. Father swore he had no idea what had become of her. He said, as wife-murderers often do, that maybe she had gone to visit relatives. He killed her that morning, after I left for school.

"He got supper for the two of us that night. Father said he would report her as a missing person to the police the next morning, if we hadn't heard from her by then. He said, 'She has been very tired and nervous lately. Have you noticed that?' "

"He was insane," said Trout. "How insane? He came into my bedroom at midnight. He woke me up. He said he had something important to tell me. It was nothing but a dirty joke, but this poor, sick man had come to believe it a parable about the awful blows that life had dealt him.

It was about a fugitive who sought shelter from the police in the home of a woman he knew.

"Her living room had a cathedral ceiling, which is to say it went all the way up to the roof peak, with rustic rafters spanning the air space below." Trout paused. It was as though he were as caught up in the tale as his father must have been.

He went on, there in the suite named in honor of the suicide Ernest Hemingway: "She was a widow, and he stripped himself naked while she went to fetch some of her husband's clothes. But before he could put them on, the police were hammering on the front door with their billy clubs. So the fugitive hid on top of a rafter. When the woman let in the police, though, his oversize testicles hung down in full view."

Trout paused again.

"The police asked the woman where the guy was. The woman said she didn't know what guy they were talking about," said Trout. "One of the cops saw the testicles hanging down from a rafter and asked what they were. She said they were Chinese temple bells. He believed her. He said he'd always wanted to hear Chinese temple bells.

"He gave them a whack with his billy club, but there was no sound. So he hit them again, a lot harder, a whole lot harder. Do you know what the guy on the rafter shrieked?" Trout asked me.

I said I didn't.

"He shrieked, 'TING-A-LING, YOU SON OF A BITCH!' "

15

The Academy should have moved its staff and treasures to a safer neighborhood when the Museum of the American Indian did so with its genocide mementos. It was still stuck way-the-hell-and-gone uptown, amid nothing but people with lives not worth living for miles in every direction, because its dwindling and demoralized membership couldn't bestir itself to OK a move.

To be perfectly frank, the only people who cared what became of the Academy were its staff, office workers, cleaning and maintenance people, and armed guards. Nor were most of them enraptured by old-fashioned art practices. They needed the jobs, no matter how pointless the work might be, and so were reminiscent of people during the Great Depression of the 1930s, who celebrated when they got any kind of work at all.

Trout characterized the sort of work he was able to get back then as "cleaning birdshit out of cuckoo clocks."

· · · · ·

The Academy's Executive Secretary certainly needed the work. Monica Pepper, who looked so much like my sister Allie, was the sole support of herself and her husband Zoltan, whom she had rendered hors de combat with a swan dive. So she had fortified the building by replacing the wooden front door with half-inch steel armorplate, fitted with a *whoozit,* or peephole, which could also be closed and locked.

She had done all she could to make the place look as abandoned and looted as the ruins of Columbia University two miles to the south. The windows, like the front door, were shuttered with steel, and the shutters were concealed in turn by rough plywood painted black and camouflaged with graffiti, which ran continuously across the whole façade. The staff had done the garish artwork. Monica herself had spray-painted "FUCK ART!" in orange and purple across the steel front door.

It so happened that an African-American armed guard named Dudley Prince was looking out through that door's *whoozit* when Trout put "The Sisters B-36" in the trash receptacle out front. Bums interacting with the receptacle were no novelty, God knows, but Trout, whom Prince mistook for a bag lady rather than a bag gentleman, put on an unusual show out there.

Here's the thing about Trout's appearance from a distance: Instead of trousers, he wore three layers of thermal underwear, revealing the shapes of his calves below the hem of his unisex war-surplus Navy overcoat. Yes, and he wore sandals rather than boots, another seemingly feminine touch, as was his babushka, fashioned from a crib blanket printed with red balloons and blue teddy bears.

Trout was out there talking to and gesturing at the lidless wire basket as though it were an editor in an old-fashioned book-publishing house, and as though his four-page handwritten yellow manuscript were a great novel, sure to sell like hotcakes. He wasn't remotely crazy. He would later say of his performance: "It was the world that had suffered the nervous breakdown. I was just having fun in a nightmare, arguing with an imaginary editor about the advertising budget, and about who should play whom in the movie, and personal appearances on TV shows and so on, perfectly harmless funny stuff."

His behavior was so outré that a genuine bag lady passing by asked him, "Are you OK, honey?"

To which Trout replied with all possible gusto, "Ting-a-ling! Ting-a-ling!"

When Trout returned to the shelter, though, the armed guard Dudley Prince unbolted the steel front door and, motivated by boredom and curiosity, retrieved the manuscript. He wanted to know what it was a bag lady, with every reason to commit suicide, one would think, had deep-sixed so ecstatically.

16

Here, for whatever it may be worth, and from *Timequake One*, is Kilgore Trout's explanation of the timequake and its aftershocks, the rerun, excerpted from his unfinished memoir *My Ten Years on Automatic Pilot*:

"The timequake of 2001 was a cosmic charley horse in the sinews of Destiny. At what was in New York City 2:27 p.m. on February 13th of that year, the Universe suffered a crisis in self-confidence. Should it go on expanding indefinitely? What was the point?

"It fibrillated with indecision. Maybe it should have a family reunion back where it all began, and then make a great big BANG again.

"It suddenly shrunk ten years. It zapped me and everybody else back to February 17th, 1991, what was for me 7:51 a.m., and a line outside a blood bank in San Diego, California.

"For reasons best known to itself, though, the Universe canceled the family reunion, for the nonce at least. It resumed expansion. Which faction, if any, cast the deciding votes on whether to expand or shrink, I cannot say. Despite my having lived for eighty-four years, or ninety-four, if you want to count the rerun, many questions about the Universe remain for me unanswered.

"That the rerun lasted ten years, short a mere four days, some are saying now, is proof that there is a God, and that He is on the Decimal System. He has ten fingers and ten toes, just as we do, they say, and uses them when He does arithmetic.

"I have my doubts. I can't help it. That's the way I am. Even if my father, the ornithologist Professor Raymond Trout of Smith College in Northampton, Massachusetts, hadn't murdered my mother, a housewife and poet, I believe I would have been that way. Then again, I have never made a serious study of the different religions, and so am unqualified to comment. About all I know for certain is that devout Muslims do not believe in Santa Claus."

On the first of the two Christmas Eves, 2000, the still religious African-American armed guard Dudley Prince thought Trout's "The Sisters B-36" just might be a message for the Academy from God Himself. What happened to the planet Booboo, after all, wasn't a whole lot different from what seemed to be happening to his own planet, and especially to his employers, what was left of the American Academy of Arts and Letters, way-the-hell-and-gone up on West 155th Street, two doors west of Broadway.

Trout got to know Prince, just as he got to know Monica Pepper and me, after the rerun ended and free will had kicked in again. Because of what the timequake had done to Prince, he had become as contemptuous of the idea of a wise and just God as my sister Allie had been. Allie opined one time, not just about her life but everybody's life, "If there is a God, He sure hates people. That's all I can say."

When Trout heard about how seriously Prince had taken "The Sisters B-36" on the first Christmas Eve, 2000, about how Prince believed a bag lady had put on such a show while throwing the yellow manuscript pages away to ensure that Prince would wonder what they were and retrieve them, the old science fiction writer commented: "Perfectly understandable, Dudley. For anybody who could believe in God, as you once did, it would be a piece of cake to believe in the planet Booboo."

Get a load of what was going to happen to Dudley Prince, a monumental figure of authority and decency in the uniform of the security company that protected the beleaguered Academy around the clock, a holstered pistol at his hip, only fifty-one days from the first of the two Christmas Eves, 2000: The timequake was going to zap him back into a solitary confinement cell, into *the hole*, within the walls and towers of the New York State Maximum Security Adult Correctional Facility at Athena, sixty miles south of his hometown of Rochester, where he used to own a little video rental store.

To be sure, the timequake had made him ten years younger, but that was no break in his case. It meant he was again serving two consecutive life sentences, without hope of parole, for the rape and murder of a ten-year-old girl of Chinese-American and Italian-American parentage, Kimberly Wang, in a Rochester crack house, of which he was entirely innocent!

Granted, at the start of the rerun Dudley Prince could remember, as could the rest of us, everything that was going to happen to him during the next ten years. He knew that in seven years he would be exonerated by DNA tests of dried ejaculate material on the victim's panties. This exculpatory evidence would again be found languishing in a glassine envelope in the walk-in vault of the District Attorney who had framed him in the hopes of being nominated for Governor.

And, oh yes, that same DA would be found wearing cement over-
shoes on the bottom of Lake Cayuga in just six more years. Prince
meanwhile was going to have to earn a High School Equivalency Certificate again, and make Jesus the center of his life again, and on and on.

And then, after he was sprung again, he would have to go on TV
talk shows again with other people who had been wrongly incarcer-
ated and then rightly exonerated, to say prison was the luckiest thing
that ever happened to him because he found Jesus there.

17

On either one of the two Christmas Eves, 2000, and it didn't matter which, except for people's opinions of what was going on, the ex-jailbird Dudley Prince delivered "The Sisters B-36" to Monica Pepper's office. Her husband Zoltan in his wheelchair was predicting the end of literacy in the not-too-distant future.

"The prophet Mohammed couldn't do it," Zoltan was saying. "Jesus, Mary, and Joseph probably couldn't do it, Mary Magdalen couldn't do it. The Emperor Charlemagne confessed he couldn't do it. It was just too hard! Nobody in the whole Western Hemisphere could do it, not even the sophisticated Mayas and Incas and Aztecs could imagine how to do it, until the Europeans came.

"Most Europeans back then couldn't read and write, either. The few who could were specialists. I promise you, sweetheart, thanks to TV that will very soon be the case again."

And then Dudley Prince said, rerun or not, "Excuse me, but I think maybe somebody is trying to tell us something."

. . . . .

Monica read "The Sisters B-36" quickly, with increasing impatience, and declared it ridiculous. She handed it to her husband. But he got no further than the name of the author before he became electrified. "My God, my God," he exclaimed, "after a quarter of a century of perfect silence, Kilgore Trout has come into my life again!"

Here's the explanation of Zoltan Pepper's reaction: When Zoltan was a high school sophomore in Fort Lauderdale, Florida, he copied a story from one of his father's collection of old science fiction magazines. He submitted it to his English teacher, Mrs. Florence Wilkerson, as his own creation. It was one of the last stories Kilgore Trout would ever submit to a publisher. By the time Zoltan was a sophomore, Trout was a bum.

The plagiarized story was about a planet in another galaxy, where the little green people, each with only one eye in the middle of his or her forehead, could get food only if they could sell goods or services to somebody else. The planet ran out of customers, and nobody could think of anything sensible to do about that. All the little green people starved to death.

Mrs. Wilkerson suspected plagiarism. Zoltan confessed, thinking it was a funny rather than a serious thing he'd done. To him, plagiarism was what Trout would have called a *mopery*, "indecent exposure in the presence of a blind person of the same sex."

Mrs. Wilkerson decided to teach Zoltan a lesson. She had him write, "I STOLE PROPERTY FROM KILGORE TROUT," on the blackboard while the class watched. Then, for the next week, she made him wear a shirt cardboard with the letter P on it, hung on his chest from around his neck, whenever he was in her classroom. She could get the piss sued out of her for doing that to a student nowadays. But then was then, and now is now.

The inspiration for what Mrs. Wilkerson did to young Zoltan Pepper was of course *The Scarlet Letter* by Nathaniel Hawthorne. In that one, a woman has to wear a big A for *adultery* on her bosom because she let a man not her husband ejaculate in her birth canal. She won't tell what his name is. He's a *preacher!*

Since Dudley Prince said it was a bag lady who had put the story in the trash receptacle out front, Zoltan didn't consider the possibility that it had been Trout himself. "It could have been his daughter or granddaughter," he speculated. "Trout himself must have died years ago. I certainly hope so, and may his soul rot in Hell."

But Trout was right next door! He was feeling just great! He was so relieved at having gotten rid of "The Sisters B-36" that he had started another story. He had been completing a story every ten days, on average, since he was fourteen. That was thirty-six a year, say. This one could have been his twenty-five-hundredth! It wasn't set on another planet. It was set in the office of a psychiatrist in St. Paul, Minnesota.

The name of the shrink was the name of the story, too, which was "Dr. Schadenfreude." This doctor had his patients lie on a couch and talk, all right, but they could ramble on only about dumb or crazy things that had happened to total strangers in supermarket tabloids or on TV talk shows.

If a patient accidentally said "I" or "me" or "my" or "myself" or "mine," Dr. Schadenfreude went ape. He leapt out of his overstuffed leather chair. He stamped his feet. He flapped his arms.

He put his livid face directly over the patient. He snarled and barked things like this: "When will you ever learn that nobody cares anything about you, you, you, you boring, insignificant piece of poop? Your whole problem is you think you *matter!* Get over that, or sashay your stuck-up butt the hell out of here!"

18

A bum on a cot next to Trout's asked him what he was writing. It was the opening paragraph of "Dr. Schadenfreude." Trout said it was a story. The bum said maybe Trout could get some money from the people next door. When Trout heard it was the American Academy of Arts and Letters next door, he said, "It might as well be a Chinese barber college as far as I'm concerned. I don't write literature. Literature is all those la-di-da monkeys next door care about.

"Those artsy-fartsy twerps next door create living, breathing, three-dimensional characters with ink on paper," he went on. "Wonderful! As though the planet weren't already dying because it has three billion too many living, breathing, three-dimensional characters!"

The only people next door, actually, of course, were Monica and Zoltan Pepper, and the three-man day shift of armed guards, headed by Dudley Prince. Monica had given her office and janitorial staffs the day off for last-minute Christmas shopping. As it happened, they were all Christian or agnostic or apostate.

The night shift of armed guards would be entirely Muslim. As

Trout would write at Xanadu, in *My Ten Years on Automatic Pilot*: "Muslims do not believe in Santa Claus."

"In my entire career as a writer," said Trout in the former Museum of the American Indian, "I created only one living, breathing, three-dimensional character. I did it with my ding-dong in a birth canal. Ting-a-ling!" He was referring to his son Leon, the deserter from the United States Marines in time of war, subsequently decapitated in a Swedish shipyard.

"If I'd wasted my time creating characters," Trout said, "I would never have gotten around to calling attention to things that really matter: irresistible forces in nature, and cruel inventions, and cockamamie ideals and governments and economies that make heroes and heroines alike feel like something the cat drug in."

Trout might have said, and it can be said of me as well, that he created *caricatures* rather than characters. His animus against so-called *mainstream literature,* moreover, wasn't peculiar to him. It was generic among writers of science fiction.

19

Strictly speaking, many of Trout's stories, except for their unbelievable characters, weren't science fiction at all. "Dr. Schadenfreude" wasn't, unless one is humorless enough to regard psychiatry as a science. The one he deposited in the Academy's trash receptacle after "Dr. Schadenfreude," with the timequake drawing ever nearer, "Bunker Bingo Party," was a roman à clef.

That one was set in Adolf Hitler's commodious bombproof bunker underneath the ruins of Berlin, Germany, at the end of World War Two in Europe. In that story, Trout calls his war, and my war, also, "Western Civilization's second unsuccessful attempt to commit suicide." He did that in conversations, too, one time adding in my presence, "If at first you don't succeed, try, try, please try again."

Tanks and infantry of the Soviet Union are only a few hundred yards away from the bunker's iron door up at street level. "Hitler, trapped below, the most loathsome human being who ever lived," wrote Trout, "doesn't know whether to shit or go blind. He is down there with his mistress Eva Braun and a few close friends, including

Joseph Goebbels, his Minister of Propaganda, and Goebbels's wife and kids."

For want of anything else remotely decisive to do, Hitler proposes marriage to Eva. She accepts!

At this point in the story, Trout asked this rhetorical question, an aside with a paragraph all to itself:

"What the heck?"

Everybody forgets his or her troubles during the marriage ceremony. After the groom kisses the bride, though, the party goes flat again. "Goebbels has a clubfoot," Trout wrote. "But Goebbels has always had a clubfoot. That is not the problem."

Goebbels remembers that his kids have brought the game of Bingo with them. It was captured intact from American troops during the Battle of the Bulge some four months earlier. I myself was captured intact during that battle. Germany, in order to conserve its resources, has stopped making its own Bingo games. Because of that, and because the grownups in the bunker have been so busy during the rise of Hitler, and now his fall, the Goebbels kids are the only ones who know how the game is played. They learned from a neighbor kid, whose family owned a prewar Bingo set.

There is this amazing scene in the story: A boy and a girl, explaining the rules of Bingo, become the center of the Universe for Nazis in full regalia, including a gaga Adolf Hitler.

That we have a copy of "Bunker Bingo Party," and copies of the four other stories Trout threw away in front of the Academy before the timequake hit, is due to Dudley Prince. The first time through, when the decade was original material, he continued to believe, as Monica Pepper did not, that a bag lady was using the trash receptacle for a mailbox, knowing he would be watching her crazy dances through the *whoozit* in the steel front door.

Prince retrieved each story and pondered it, hoping to discover some important message from a higher power encoded therein. After work, rerun or not, this was a lonely African-American.

20

In the summer of 2001 at Xanadu, Dudley Prince handed Trout the sheaf of stories, which Trout had expected the Department of Sanitation to incinerate or bury or drop in the ocean far offshore before anyone other than himself had read them. By his own account to me, Trout riffled through the scruffy pages with distaste, while seated tailor-fashion and naked on his king-size bed in the Ernest Hemingway Suite. The day was hot. He was fresh from his Jacuzzi.

But then his gaze fell upon the scene in which two anti-Semitic children teach Bingo to high-ranking Nazis in their madly theatrical uniforms. In amazed admiration for something brilliant he himself had written, and Trout had never thought of himself as worth a hill of beans as a writer, he praised the scene as an echo of this prophecy from the Book of Isaiah:

"The wolf also shall dwell with the lamb, and the leopard shall lie down with the kid; and the calf and the young lion and the fatling together; and a little child shall lead them."

. . . . .

A *fatling* is any young animal fattened for slaughter.

"I read that scene," Trout told me and Monica, "and I asked myself, 'How the hell did I *do* that?'"

That wasn't the first time I'd heard a person who had done a remarkable piece of work ask that delightful question. Back in the 1960s, long, long before the timequake, I had a great big old house in Barnstable Village on Cape Cod, where my first wife, Jane Marie Vonnegut, née Cox, and I were raising four boys and two girls. The ell where I did my writing was falling down.

I had it pulled all the way down and hauled away. I hired my friend Ted Adler, a skilled man-of-all-work my age, to build me a new one like the old one. Ted alone built the forms for the footings. Ted supervised the pouring of concrete from a ready-mix truck. He personally laid concrete blocks atop the footings. He framed the superstructure, put on the sheathing and siding, and shingled the roof and wired the place. He hung the windows and doors. He nailed up and jointed the Sheetrock inside.

The Sheetrock was the last step. I myself would do the exterior and interior painting. I told Ted I wanted to do at least that much, or he would have done that, too. When he himself had finished, and he had taken all the scraps I didn't want for kindling to the dump, he had me stand next to him outside and look at my new ell from thirty feet away.

And then he asked it: "How the hell did I *do* that?"

That question remains for me in the summer of 1996 one of my three favorite quotations. Two of the three are questions rather than good advice of any kind. The second is Jesus Christ's "Who is it they say I am?"

The third is from my son Mark, pediatrician and watercolorist and sax player. I've already quoted him in another book: "We are here to help each other get through this thing, whatever it is."

One might protest, "My dear Dr. Vonnegut, we can't all be pediatricians."

In "Bunker Bingo Party," the Nazis participate in Bingo, with the Minister of Propaganda, arguably the most effective communicator in history, calling out the coordinates of winning or losing squares on the players' cards. The game proves as analgesic for war criminals in deep doodoo as it continues to be for harmless old biddies at church fairs.

Several of the war criminals wear an Iron Cross, awarded only to Germans who have demonstrated battlefield fearlessness so excessive as to be classifiable as psychopathic. Hitler wears one. He won it as a corporal in Western Civilization's first unsuccessful attempt to commit suicide.

I was a PFC during the second botched effort to end it all. Like Ernest Hemingway, I never shot a human being. Maybe Hitler never did that big trick, either. He didn't get his country's highest decoration for killing a lot of people. He got it for being such a brave messenger. Not everybody on a battlefield is supposed to concentrate on nothing but killing. I myself was an intelligence and reconnaissance scout, going places our side hadn't occupied, looking for enemies. I wasn't supposed to fight them if I found them. I was supposed to stay unnoticed and alive, so I could tell my superiors where they were, and what it looked like they were doing.

It was wintertime, and I myself was awarded my country's second-lowest decoration, a Purple Heart for frostbite.

· · · · ·

When I got home from my war, my uncle Dan clapped me on the back, and he bellowed, "You're a *man* now!"

I damn near killed my first German.

To return to Trout's roman à clef: As though there were a God in Heaven after all, it is Der Führer who shouts "BINGO!" Adolf Hitler wins! He says incredulously, in German, of course, "I can't believe it. I've never played this game before, and yet I've won, I've *won*! What can this be but a miracle?" He is a Roman Catholic.

He rises from his chair at the table. His eyes are still fixed on the winning card before him, according to Trout, "as if it were a shred from the Shroud of Turin." This prick asks, "What can this mean but that things aren't as bad as we thought they were?"

Eva Braun spoils the moment by swallowing a capsule of cyanide. Goebbels's wife gave it to her for a wedding present. Frau Goebbels had more capsules than she needed for her immediate family. Trout wrote of Eva Braun, "Her only crime was to have allowed a monster to ejaculate in her birth canal. These things happen to the best of women."

A Communistic 240-millimeter howitzer shell explodes atop the bunker. Flakes of calcimine from the shaken ceiling shower down on the deafened occupants. Hitler himself makes a joke, demonstrating that he still has his sense of humor. "It snows," he says. That is a poetic way of saying, too, it is high time he killed himself, unless he wants to become a caged superstar in a traveling freak show, along with the bearded lady and the geek.

He puts a pistol to his head. Everybody says, *"Nein, nein, nein."* He convinces everyone that shooting himself is the dignified thing to do. What should his last words be? He says, "How about 'I regret nothing'?"

Goebbels replies that such a statement would be appropriate, but that the Parisian cabaret performer Edith Piaf has made a worldwide reputation by singing those same words in French for decades. "Her sobriquet," says Goebbels, "is 'Little Sparrow.' You don't want to be remembered as a little sparrow, or I miss my guess."

Hitler still hasn't lost his sense of humor. He says, "How about 'BINGO'?"

But he is tired. He puts the pistol to his head again. He says, "I never asked to be born in the first place."

The pistol goes "BANG!"

21

I am Honorary President of the American Humanist Association, whose headquarters in Amherst, New York, I have never seen. I succeeded the late author and biochemist Dr. Isaac Asimov in that functionless capacity. That we have an organization, a boring business, is to let others know we are numerous. We would prefer to live our lives as Humanists and not talk about it, or think more about it than we think about breathing.

Humanists try to behave decently and honorably without any expectation of rewards or punishments in an afterlife. The creator of the Universe has been to us unknowable so far. We serve as well as we can the highest abstraction of which we have some understanding, which is our community.

Are we enemies of members of organized religions? No. My great war buddy Bernard V. O'Hare, now dead, lost his faith as a Roman Catholic during World War Two. I didn't like that. I thought that was too much to lose.

I had never had faith like that, because I had been raised by interesting and moral people who, like Thomas Jefferson and Benjamin Franklin, were nonetheless skeptics about what preachers said was going on. But I knew Bernie had lost something important and honorable.

Again, I did not like that, did not like it because I liked *him* so much.

I spoke at a Humanist Association memorial service for Dr. Asimov a few years back. I said, "Isaac is up in Heaven now." That was the funniest thing I could have said to an audience of Humanists. I rolled them in the aisles. The room was like the court-martial scene in Trout's "No Laughing Matter," right before the floor of the Pacific Ocean swallowed up the third atomic bomb and *Joy's Pride* and all the rest of it.

When I myself am dead, God forbid, I hope some wag will say about me, "He's up in Heaven now."

I like to sleep. I published a new requiem for old music in another book, in which I said it was no bad thing to want sleep for everyone as an afterlife.

I see no need up in the sky for more torture chambers and Bingo games.

Yesterday, Wednesday, July 3rd, 1996, I received a well-written letter from a man who never asked to be born in the first place, and who has been a captive of our nonpareil correctional facilities, first as a juvenile offender and then as an adult offender, for many years. He is about to be released into a world where he has no friends or relatives. Free will is about to kick in again, after a hiatus of a good deal more than a decade. What should he do?

I, Honorary President of the American Humanist Association, wrote back today, "Join a church." I said this because what such a grown-up waif needs more than anything is something like a family.

I couldn't recommend Humanism for such a person. I wouldn't do so for the great majority of the planet's population.

The German philosopher Friedrich Wilhelm Nietzsche, who had syphilis, said that only a person of deep faith could afford the luxury of religious skepticism. Humanists, by and large educated, comfortably middle-class persons with rewarding lives like mine, find rapture enough in secular knowledge and hope. Most people can't.

Voltaire, French author of *Candide,* and therefore the Humanists' Abraham, concealed his contempt for the hierarchy of the Roman Catholic Church from his less educated, simpler-minded, and more frightened employees, because he knew what a stabilizer their religion was for them.

With some trepidation, I told Trout in the summer of 2001 about my advice to the man soon to be expelled from prison. He asked if I had heard from this person again, if I knew what had become of him in the intervening five years, or in the intervening ten years, if we wanted to count the rerun. I hadn't and didn't.

He asked if I myself had ever tried to join a church, just for the hell of it, to find out what that was like. *He* had. The closest I ever came to that, I said, was when my second-wife-to-be, Jill Krementz, and I thought it would be cute, and also ritzy, to be married in the Little Church Around the Corner, a Disneyesque Episcopal house of worship on East Twenty-ninth Street off Fifth Avenue in Manhattan.

"When they found out I was a divorced person," I said, "they pre-

cribedof

scribed all sorts of penitent services I was to perform before I was clean enough to be married there."

"There you are," said Trout. "Imagine all the chickenshit you'd have to go through if you were an ex-con. And if that poor son of a bitch who wrote you really did find a church to accept him, he could easily be back in prison."

"For what?" I said. "For robbing the poor box?"

"No," said Trout, "for delighting Jesus Christ by shooting dead a doctor coming to work in an abortion mill."

22

I forget what I was doing on the afternoon of February 13th, 2001, when the timequake struck. It couldn't have been much. I sure as heck wasn't writing another book. I was seventy-eight, for heaven's sakes! My daughter Lily was eighteen!

Old Kilgore Trout was still writing, though. Seated on his cot at the shelter, where everybody thought his name was Vincent van Gogh, he had just begun a story about a working-class Londoner, Albert Hardy, also the name of the story. Albert Hardy was born in 1896, with his head between his legs, and his genitalia sprouting out of the top of his neck, which looked "like a zucchini."

Albert's parents taught him to walk on his hands and eat with his feet. That was so they could conceal his private parts with trousers. The private parts weren't excessively large like the testicles of the fugitive in Trout's father's Ting-a-ling parable. That wasn't the point.

Monica Pepper was at her desk next door, only feet away, but they still hadn't met. She and Dudley Prince and her husband still believed the depositor of stories in the trash receptacle out front was an old woman, so she couldn't possibly live next door. Their best guess was that she came from the shelter for battered old people over on Convent Avenue, or the detox center in the parish house down at the Cathedral of Saint John the Divine, which was unisex.

Monica's own home, and Zoltan's, was an apartment down in Turtle Bay, a safe neighborhood seven miles away, comfortably close to the United Nations. She came and went from work in her own chauffeur-driven limousine, which was modified to accommodate Zoltan's wheelchair. The Academy was fabulously well-to-do. Money was not a problem. Thanks to lavish gifts from old-fashioned art lovers in the past, it was richer than several members of the United Nations, including, surely, Mali, Swaziland, and Luxembourg.

Zoltan had the limo that afternoon. He was on his way to pick up Monica. She was awaiting Zoltan's arrival when the timequake struck. He would get as far as ringing the Academy doorbell before he was zapped back to February 17th, 1991. He would be ten years younger and *whole* again!

Talk about getting a reaction from a doorbell!

When the rerun was over, though, and free will kicked in again, everybody and everything were exactly where they had been when the timequake struck. So Zoltan was paraplegic again in a wheelchair, ringing the doorbell again. He didn't realize that it was all of a sudden up to him to decide what his finger was going to do next. His finger, for want of instructions from him or anything else, went on ringing and ringing the doorbell.

That's what it was doing when Zoltan was smacked by a runaway fire truck. The driver of the truck hadn't realized yet that it was up to him to *steer* the thing.

· · · · ·

77

As Trout wrote in *My Ten Years on Automatic Pilot*: "It was free will that did all the damage. The timequake and its aftershocks didn't snap as much as a single strand in a spider's web, unless some other force had snapped that strand the first time through."

Monica was working on the budget for Xanadu when the timequake struck. The endowment of that writers' retreat up in Point Zion, Rhode Island, the Julius King Bowen Foundation, was administered by the Academy. Julius King Bowen, who died before Monica was born, was a never-married white man who made a fortune during the 1920s and early 1930s with stories and lectures about the hilarious, but touching, too, efforts by American black people to imitate successful American white people, so they could be successful, too.

A cast-iron historical marker on the border between Point Zion's public beach and Xanadu said the mansion had been Bowen's home and place of work from 1922 until his death in 1936. It said President Warren G. Harding had proclaimed Bowen "Laughter Laureate of the United States, Master of Darky Dialects, and Heir to the Crown of King of Humor Once Worn by Mark Twain."

As Trout would point out to me when I read that marker in 2001: "Warren G. Harding sired an illegitimate daughter by ejaculating in the birth canal of a stenographer in a broom closet at the White House."

23

When Trout was zapped back to a line outside a blood bank in San Diego, California, in 1991, he could remember how his story about the guy with his head between his legs and his ding-dong atop his neck, "Albert Hardy," would end. But he couldn't write that finale for ten years, until free will kicked in again. Albert Hardy would be blown to pieces while a soldier in the Second Battle of the Somme in World War One.

Albert Hardy's dogtags wouldn't be found. His body parts would be reassembled as though he had been like everybody else, with his head atop his neck. He couldn't be given back his ding-dong. To be perfectly frank, his ding-dong wouldn't have been what you might call the subject of an exhaustive search.

Albert Hardy would be buried under an Eternal Flame in France, in the Tomb of the Unknown Soldier, "normal at last."

I myself was zapped back to this house near the tip of Long Island, New York, where I am writing now, halfway through the rerun. In

1991, as now, I was gazing at a list of all I'd published, and wondering, "How the hell did I *do* that?"

I was feeling as I feel now, like whalers Herman Melville described, who didn't talk anymore. They had said absolutely everything they could ever say.

I told Trout in 2001 about a redheaded boyhood friend of mine, David Craig, now a builder in New Orleans, Louisiana, who won a Bronze Star in our war for knocking out a German tank in Normandy. He and a buddy came upon this steel monster parked all alone in a woods. Its engine wasn't running. There wasn't anybody outside. A radio was playing popular music inside.

Dave and his buddy fetched a bazooka. When they got back, the tank was still there. A radio was still playing music inside. They shot the tank with the bazooka. Germans didn't pop out of the turret. The radio stopped playing. That was all. That was it.

Dave and his buddy skedaddled away from there.

Trout said it sounded to him as though my boyhood friend's Bronze Star was well deserved. "He almost certainly killed people as well as a radio," he said, "thus sparing them years of disappointments and tedium in civilian life. He made it possible for them, to quote the English poet A. E. Housman, to 'die in their glory and never be old.' "

Trout paused, secured his upper plate with his left thumb, and then went on: "I could have written a best-seller, if I'd had the patience to create three-dimensional characters. The Bible may be the Greatest Story Ever Told, but the most popular story you can ever tell is about a good-looking couple having a really swell time copulating outside wedlock, and having to quit for one reason or another while doing it is still a novelty."

I was reminded of Steve Adams, one of my sister Allie's three sons my first wife Jane and I adopted after Allie's unlucky husband Jim died in a railroad train that went off an open drawbridge in New Jersey, and then, two days later, Allie died of cancer of the everything.

When Steve came home to Cape Cod for Christmas vacation from his freshman year at Dartmouth, he was close to tears because he had just read, having been forced to do so by a professor, *A Farewell to Arms*, by Ernest Hemingway.

Steve, now a middle-aged comedy writer for movies and TV, was so gorgeously wrecked back then that I was moved to reread what it was that had done this to him. *A Farewell to Arms* turned out to be an attack on the institution of marriage. Hemingway's hero is wounded in war. He and his nurse fall in love. They honeymoon far away from the battlefields, consuming the best food and wine, without having been married first. She gets pregnant, proving, as if it could be doubted, that he is indeed all man.

She and the baby die, so he doesn't have to get a regular job and a house and life insurance and all that crap, and he has such beautiful memories.

I said to Steve, "The tears Hemingway has made you want to shed are tears of *relief*! It looked like the guy was going to have to get married and settle down. But then he didn't have to. Whew! What a close shave!"

· · · · ·

Trout said he could think of only one other book that despised matrimony as much as *A Farewell to Arms*.

"Name it," I said.

He said it was a book by Henry David Thoreau, called *Walden*.

"Loved it," I said.

24

I say in lectures in 1996 that fifty percent or more of American marriages go bust because most of us no longer have extended families. When you marry somebody now, all you get is one person.

I say that when couples fight, it isn't about money or sex or power. What they're really saying is, "You're not enough people!"

Sigmund Freud said he didn't know what women wanted. I know what women want. They want a whole lot of people to talk to.

I thank Trout for the concept of the *man-woman hour* as a unit of measurement of marital intimacy. This is an hour during which a husband and wife are close enough to be aware of each other, and for one to say something to the other without yelling, if he or she feels like it. Trout says in his story "Golden Wedding" that they needn't feel like saying anything in order to credit themselves with a man-woman hour.

"Golden Wedding" is another story Dudley Prince rescued from the trash receptacle before the timequake. It is about a florist who tries to increase his business by convincing people who both work at home, or who spend long hours together running a Ma-and-Pa joint, that they are entitled to celebrate several wedding anniversaries a year.

He calculates that an average couple with separate places of work logs four man-woman hours each weekday, and sixteen of them on weekends. Being sound asleep with each other doesn't count. This gives him a standard *man-woman week* of thirty-six man-woman hours.

He multiplies that by fifty-two. This gives him, when rounded off, a standard *man-woman year* of eighteen hundred man-woman hours. He advertises that any couple that has accumulated this many man-woman hours is entitled to celebrate an anniversary, and to receive flowers and appropriate presents, even if it took them only twenty weeks to do it!

If couples keep piling up man-woman hours like that, as my wives and I have done in both my marriages, they can easily celebrate their Ruby Anniversary in only twenty years, and their Golden in twenty-five!

I do not propose to discuss my love life. I will say that I still can't get over how women are shaped, and that I will go to my grave wanting to pet their butts and boobs. I will say, too, that lovemaking, if sincere, is one of the best ideas Satan put in the apple she gave to the serpent to give to Eve. The best idea in that apple, though, is making jazz.

25

Allie's husband Jim Adams really did go off an open drawbridge in a railroad train two days before Allie died in a hospital. Stranger than fiction!

Jim had plunged them deep in debt by manufacturing a toy of his own invention. It was a corked rubber balloon with a blob of permanently malleable clay inside. It was clay with a skin!

The face of a clown was printed on the balloon. You could make it open its mouth wide with your fingers, or make its nose protrude or its eyes sink in. Jim called it Putty Puss. Putty Puss never became popular. Moreover, Putty Puss amassed enormous debts for its manufacture and advertising.

Allie and Jim, Indianapolis people in New Jersey, had four boys and no girls. One of the boys was a mewling infant, and none of these people had asked to be born in the first place.

Boys and girls of our family often come into this world, as did Allie, with natural gifts for drawing and painting and sculpting and so on.

Jane's and my two daughters, Edith and Nanette, are middle-aged professional artists who have shows and sell pictures. So does our son the doctor Mark. So do I. Allie could have done that, too, if she had been willing to work hard and hustle some. But as I have reported elsewhere, she said, "Just because you're talented, that doesn't mean you have to *do* something with it."

I say in my novel *Bluebeard,* "Beware of gods bearing gifts." I think I had Allie in mind when I wrote that, and Allie in mind again when, in *Timequake One,* I had Monica Pepper spray-paint "FUCK ART!" in orange and purple across the steel front door of the Academy. Allie didn't know there was such an institution as the Academy, I'm almost sure, but she would have been happy to see those words emblazoned anywhere.

Our father the architect was so full of ecstatic baloney about any work of art Allie made when she was growing up, as though she were the new Michelangelo, that she was shamed. She wasn't stupid and she wasn't tasteless. Father, without meaning to do so, rubbed her nose in how limited her gifts were, and so spoiled any modest pleasure that she, not expecting too much, might have found in using them.

Allie may have felt patronized, too, lavishly praised for very little because she was a pretty girl. Only men could become great artists.

When I was ten, and Allie was fifteen, and our big brother Bernie the born scientist was eighteen, I said at supper one night that women weren't even the best cooks or clothing makers. Men were. And Mother dumped a pitcher of water over my head.

But Mother was as full of baloney about Allie's prospects for marrying a rich man, and how important it was for Allie to do so, as Father was about the art she did. During the Great Depression, financial sacrifices were made to send Allie to school with Hoosier heiresses at Tudor Hall, School for Girls, or *Two-Door Hell, Dump for Dames,* four blocks south of Shortridge High School, where she could have received what I received, a free and much richer and more democratic and madly heterosexual education.

The parents of my first wife Jane, Harvey and Riah Cox, did the same thing: sent their only daughter to Tudor Hall, and bought her rich girls' clothes, and maintained for her sake membership in the Woodstock Golf and Country Club they could ill afford, so she could marry a man whose family had money and power.

When the Great Depression and then World War Two were over, the idea that a man from a rich and powerful Indianapolis family would be allowed to marry a woman whose family didn't have a pot to piss in, as long as she had the manners and tastes of a rich girl, turned out to be as dumb as trying to sell balloons with blobs of moistened clay inside.

Business is business.

The best Allie could do for a husband was Jim Adams, a beautiful, charming, funny hunk with no money and no profession, who had served in Army Public Relations during the war. The best Jane could do, and it was a time of panic for unmarried women, was a guy who came home a PFC, who had been flunking all his courses at Cornell when he went off to war, and who didn't have a clue as to what to do next, now that free will had kicked in again.

Get this: Not only did Jane have rich girls' manners and clothes. She was a Phi Beta Kappa from Swarthmore, and had been the outstanding writer there!

I thought maybe I could be some kind of half-assed scientist, since that had been my education.

26

In the third edition of *The Oxford Dictionary of Quotations*, the English poet Samuel Taylor Coleridge (1772–1834) speaks of "that willing suspension of disbelief for the moment, which constitutes poetic faith." This acceptance of balderdash is essential to the enjoyment of poems, and of novels and short stories, and of dramas, too. Some assertions by writers, however, are simply too preposterous to be believed.

Who, for example, could believe Kilgore Trout when he wrote as follows in *My Ten Years on Automatic Pilot*: "There is a planet in the Solar System where the people are so stupid they didn't catch on for a million years that there was another half to their planet. They didn't figure that out until five hundred years ago! Only five hundred years ago! And yet they are now calling themselves *Homo sapiens*.

"Dumb? You want to talk dumb? The people in one of the halves were so dumb, they didn't have an alphabet! They hadn't invented the wheel yet!"

Give us a break, Mr. Trout.

· · · · ·

He appears to be heaping scorn in particular on Native Americans, who have already been adequately penalized, one would think, for their stupidity. According to Noam Chomsky, a professor at the Massachusetts Institute of Technology, where my brother, my father, and my grandfather all earned advanced degrees, but where my maternal uncle Pete Lieber flunked out: "Current estimates suggest that there may have been about 80 million Native Americans in Latin America when Columbus 'discovered' the continent—as we say—and about 12 to 15 million more north of the Rio Grande."

Chomsky continues: "By 1650, about 95 percent of the population of Latin America had been wiped out, and by the time the continental borders of the United States had been established, some 200,000 were left of the indigenous population."

In my opinion, Trout, far from giving yet another high colonic to our aborigines, is raising the question, perhaps too subtly, of whether great discoveries, such as the existence of another hemisphere, or of accessible atomic energy, really make people any happier than they were before.

I myself say atomic energy has made people unhappier than they were before, and that having to live in a two-hemisphere planet has made our aborigines a lot less happy, without making the wheel-and-alphabet people who "discovered" them any fonder of being alive than they were before.

Then again, I am a monopolar depressive descended from monopolar depressives. That's how come I write so good.

Are two hemispheres better than one? I know anecdotal evidence isn't worth a pitcher of warm spit scientifically, but a great-grandfather of mine on my mother's side switched hemispheres in time to be wounded in the leg as a soldier for the Union in our notoriously uncivil Civil War. His name was Peter Lieber. Peter Lieber bought a brewery in Indianapolis, and it prospered. A brew of his won a Gold Medal at the Paris Exposition of 1889. Its secret ingredient was coffee.

But Peter Lieber gave the brewery to his son Albert, my maternal grandfather, and he went back to his original hemisphere. He decided he liked that one better. And I am told there is a photograph often used in our textbooks that supposedly shows immigrants disembarking here, but actually they are getting on a ship to go back to where they came from.

This hemisphere is no bed of roses. My mother committed suicide in this one, and then my brother-in-law went off an open drawbridge in a railroad train.

27

The first story Trout had to rewrite after the timequake zapped him back to 1991, he told me, was called "Dog's Breakfast." It was about a mad scientist named Fleon Sunoco, who was doing research at the National Institutes of Health in Bethesda, Maryland. Dr. Sunoco believed really smart people had little radio receivers in their heads, and were getting their bright ideas from somewhere else.

"The smarties *had to be getting outside help*," Trout said to me at Xanadu. While impersonating the mad Sunoco, Trout himself seemed convinced that there was a great big computer somewhere, which, by means of radio, had told Pythagoras about right triangles, and Newton about gravity, and Darwin about evolution, and Pasteur about germs, and Einstein about relativity, and on and on.

"That computer, wherever it is, whatever it is, while pretending to help us, may actually be trying to *kill* us dummies with too much to think about," said Kilgore Trout.

. . . . .

Trout said he hadn't minded writing "Dog's Breakfast" again, or the three hundred or more stories he redid and threw away before free will kicked in again. "Write or rewrite, it's all the same to me," he said. "At the age of four score and four, I am as amazed and entertained as I was when I was only fourteen, and discovered that if I put the tip of a pen on paper, it would write a story of its own accord.

"Wonder why I tell people that my name is Vincent van Gogh?" he asked. And I had better explain that the real Vincent van Gogh was a Dutchman who painted in the south of France, whose pictures are now numbered among the world's most precious treasures, but who in his own lifetime sold only two of them. "It isn't only because he, like me, took no pride in his appearance and disgusted women, although that surely has to be factored in," said Trout.

"The main thing about van Gogh and me," said Trout, "is that he painted pictures that astonished *him* with their importance, even though nobody else thought they were worth a damn, and I write stories that astonish *me*, even though nobody else thinks they're worth a damn.

"How lucky can you get?"

Trout was the only appreciative audience he needed for what he was and did. That let him accept the conditions of the rerun as unsurprising. It was just more foolishness in the world outside his own, and no more worthy of his respect than wars or economic collapses or plagues, or tidal waves, or TV stars, or what you will.

He was capable of being such a rational hero in the neighborhood of the Academy the instant free will kicked in again, because, in my opinion, Trout, unlike most of the rest of us, had found no significant differences between life as déjà vu and life as original material.

As for how little he was affected by the rerun, as compared with the hell it had been for most of the rest of us, he wrote in *My Ten Years on*

Automatic Pilot: "I didn't need a timequake to teach me being alive was a crock of shit. I already knew that from my childhood and crucifixes and history books."

For the record: Dr. Fleon Sunoco at the NIH, who is independently rich, hires grave robbers to bring him the brains of deceased members of Mensa, a nationwide club for persons with high Intelligence Quotients, or IQs, as determined by standardized tests of verbal and non-verbal skills, tests which pit the testees against the Joe and Jane Sixpacks, against the *Lumpenproletariat*.

His ghouls also bring him brains of people who died in really stupid accidents, crossing busy streets against the light, starting charcoal fires at cookouts with gasoline, and so on, for comparison. So as not to arouse suspicion, they deliver the fresh brains one at a time in buckets stolen from a nearby Kentucky Fried Chicken franchise. Needless to say, Sunoco's supervisors have no idea what he's really doing when he works late night after night.

They *do* notice how much he likes fried chicken, apparently, ordering it by the bucket, and that he never offers anybody else some. They also wonder how he stays so skinny. During regular working hours, he does what he is paid to do, which is develop a birth control pill that takes all the pleasure out of sex, so teenagers won't copulate.

At night, though, with nobody around, he slices up high-IQ brains, looking for little radios. He doesn't think Mensa members had them inserted surgically. He thinks they were *born* with them, so the receivers have to be made of meat. Sunoco has written in his secret journal: "There is no way an unassisted human brain, which is nothing more than a dog's breakfast, three and a half pounds of blood-soaked sponge, could have written 'Stardust,' let alone Beethoven's Ninth Symphony."

. . . . .

One night he finds an unexplained little snot-colored bump, no larger than a mustard seed, in the inner ear of a Mensa member, who as a junior high schooler had won spelling bee after spelling bee. *Eureka!*

He reexamines the inner ear of a moron who was killed when she was grabbing door handles of fast-moving vehicles while wearing Rollerblades. Neither of her inner ears has a snot-colored bump. *Eureka!*

Sunoco examines fifty more brains, half from people so stupid you couldn't believe it, half from people so smart you couldn't believe it. Only the inner ears of the rocket scientists, so to speak, have bumps. The bumps *have to have been the reason* the smarties were so good at taking IQ tests. An extra piece of tissue that little, and as nothing but tissue, couldn't possibly have been much more help than a pimple. It has to be a radio! And radios like that have to be feeding correct answers to questions, no matter how recondite, to Mensas and Phi Beta Kappas, and to quiz show contestants.

This is a Nobel Prize–type discovery! So, even before he has published, Fleon Sunoco goes out and buys himself a suit of tails for Stockholm.

28

Trout said: "Fleon Sunoco jumped to his death into the National Institutes of Health parking lot. He was wearing his new suit of tails, which would never get to Stockholm.

"He realized that his discovery proved that he didn't deserve credit for making it. He was hoist by his own petard! Anybody who did anything as wonderful as what he had done couldn't possibly have done it with just a human brain, with nothing but the dog's breakfast in his braincase. He could have done it only with outside help."

When free will kicked in after a ten-year hiatus, Trout made the transition from déjà vu to unlimited opportunities almost seamlessly. The rerun brought him back to the point in the space-time continuum when he was again beginning his story about the British soldier whose head was where his ding-dong should have been and whose ding-dong was where his head should have been.

Without warning and silently, the rerun stopped.

This was one heck of a moment for anyone operating a form of self-propelled transportation, or who was a passenger in one, or who stood in the path of one. For ten years, machinery, like people, had been doing whatever it had done the first time through the decade, often with fatal results, to be sure. As Trout wrote in *My Ten Years on Automatic Pilot:* "Rerun or not, modern transportation is a game of inches." The second time through, though, the hiccuping Universe, not humanity, was responsible for any and all fatalities. People might look as though they were steering something, but they weren't really steering. They couldn't steer.

Quoting Trout again: "The horse knew the way home." But when the rerun ended, the horse, which might actually have been anything from a motor scooter to a jumbo jet, didn't know the way home anymore. People were going to have to tell it what to do next, if it wasn't going to be an utterly amoral plaything of Newton's Laws of Motion.

Trout, on his cot next door to the Academy, was operating nothing more dangerous or headstrong than a ballpoint pen. When free will kicked in, he simply went on writing. He finished the story. The wings of a narrative, begging to be told, had carried its author over what was for most of us a yawning abyss.

Only after he had completed his own absorbing business, the story, was Trout at liberty to notice what the outside world, or, indeed, the Universe, might be doing now, if anything. And as a man without a culture or a society, he was uniquely free to apply Occam's Razor, or, if you like, the Law of Parsimony, to virtually any situation, to wit: The simplest explanation of a phenomenon is, nine times out of ten, say, truer than a really fancy one.

Trout's ruminations about how he had been able to finish a story whose completion had been so long opposed were uncomplicated by conventional paradigms of what life was all about, and what the Universe can or cannot do, and so on. Thus was the old science fiction writer able to go directly to this simple truth: That everybody had been going through what he had been going through for the past ten years, that he hadn't gone nuts or died and gone to hell, and that the Universe had shrunk a little bit, but had then resumed expansion, making everybody and everything a robot of their own past, and demonstrating, incidentally, that the past was unmalleable and indestructible, to wit:

The Moving Finger writes; and, having writ,
Moves on: nor all your Piety nor Wit
Shall lure it back to cancel half a Line,
Nor all your Tears wash out a Word of it.

And then, on what was the afternoon of February 13th, 2001, in New York City, way-the-hell-and-gone up on West 155th Street, and *everywhere*, free will had all of a sudden kicked in again.

29

I, too, went from déjà vu to unlimited opportunities in a series of actions that were continuous. An outside observer might have said I exercised free will the instant it became available. But here's the thing: I had dumped a cup of very hot chicken noodle soup into my lap, and had jumped out of my chair, and was with my bare hands sweeping the scalding broth and noodles from the front of my trousers right before the timequake struck. That's what I had to be doing again at the end of the rerun.

When free will kicked in, I simply kept on trying to get the soup off me before it could seep all the way through to my underwear. Trout said, quite correctly, that my actions had been *reflexes*, and not sufficiently creative to be considered acts of free will.

"If you'd been thinking," he said, "you would have unzipped your pants and dropped them around your ankles, since they were already soaked with soup. No amount of frenzied brushing of the surface of your pants was going to stop the soup from seeping all the way through to your underwear."

· · · · ·

Trout was surely among the first people in the whole wide world, and not just way-the-hell-and-gone up on West 155th Street, to realize that free will had kicked in. This was very interesting to him, as it certainly wasn't to many others. Most other people, after the relentless reprise of their mistakes and bad luck and hollow victories during the past ten years, had, in Trout's words, "stopped giving a shit what was going on, or what was liable to happen next." This syndrome would eventually be given a name: *Post-Timequake Apathy*, or *PTA*.

Trout now performed an experiment that many of us had tried to perform at the start of the rerun. He said nonsensical things on purpose, and out loud, like, "Boop-boop-a-doop, dingle-dangle, artsy-fartsy, wah, wah," and so on. We all tried to say things on that order back in the second 1991, hoping to prove we could still say or do whatever we liked, if we tried hard enough. We couldn't, of course. But when Trout tried to say, "Blue mink bifocals," or whatever, *after* the rerun, of course he could.

No problem!

People in Europe and Africa and Asia were in darkness when free will kicked in. Most of them were in bed or sitting down somewhere. Not nearly as many of them fell down in their hemisphere as fell down in ours, where a clear majority was wide awake.

A person walking in either hemisphere was commonly off balance, leaning in the direction he or she was going, and with most of his or her weight unevenly distributed between his or her feet. When free will kicked in, he or she of course fell down, and stayed down, even in the middle of a street with onrushing traffic, because of Post-Timequake Apathy.

You can imagine what the bottoms of staircases and escalators, in the Western Hemisphere in particular, looked like after free will kicked in.

That's the *New World* for you!

My sister Allie in real life, which for her lasted only forty-one years, God rest her soul, thought falling down was one of the funniest things people could do. I don't mean people who fell on account of strokes or heart attacks or snapped hamstrings or whatever. I am talking about people ten years old or older, of any race and either sex, and in reasonably good physical condition, who, on a day like any other day, all of a sudden fell down.

When Allie was dying for sure, with not long to go, I could still fill her with joy, could give her an *epiphany*, if you like, by talking about somebody falling down. My story couldn't be from the movies or hearsay. It had to be about a rude reminder of the power of gravity that I myself had witnessed.

Only one of my stories was about a professional entertainer. It was from back when I was lucky enough to see the death throes of vaudeville on the stage of the Apollo Theater in Indianapolis. A perfectly wonderful man, my kind of saint, as a regular part of his act at one point fell into the orchestra pit, and then climbed back onto the stage wearing the big bass drum.

All my other stories, which Allie never tired of hearing until she was dead as a doornail, involved *amateurs*.

30

One time when Allie was maybe fifteen and I was ten, she heard somebody fall down our basement stairs: *Bloompity, bloomp, bloomp.* She thought it was I, so she stood at the top of the stairs laughing her fool head off. This would have been 1932, three years into the Great Depression.

But it wasn't I. It was a guy from the gas company, who had come to read the meter. He came clumping out of the basement all bunged up, and absolutely furious.

Another time, when Allie was sixteen or older, since she was driving a car with me as a passenger, we saw a woman come out of a stopped streetcar horizontally, headfirst and parallel to the pavement. Her heels had caught somehow.

As I've written elsewhere, and said in interviews, Allie and I laughed for years about that woman. She wasn't seriously hurt. She got back on her feet OK.

One thing that only I saw, but which Allie liked to hear about anyhow, was a guy who offered to teach a beautiful woman not his wife how to do the Tango. It was at the tail end of a cocktail party that had pretty much petered out.

I don't think the man's wife was there. I can't imagine he would have made the offer if his wife had been there. He was not a professional dance instructor. There were maybe ten people in all there, including the host and hostess. This was in the days of phonographs. The host and hostess had made the tactical mistake of putting an acetate recording of Tango music on their phonograph.

So this guy, his eyes flashing, his nostrils flaring, took this beautiful woman in his arms, and he fell down.

Yes, and all the people falling down in *Timequake One,* and now in this book, are like "FUCK ART!" spray-painted across the steel front door of the Academy. They are homage to my sister Allie. They are Allie's kind of porno: people deprived of dignified postures by gravity instead of sex.

Here is a verse from a song popular during the Great Depression:

> *Papa came home late last night.*
> *Mama said, "Pop, you're tight."*
> *When he tried to find the light,*
> *He faw down and go boom!*

That the impulse to laugh at healthy people who nonetheless fall down is by no means universal, however, was brought to my attention unpleasantly at a performance of *Swan Lake* by the Royal Ballet in London, England. I was in the audience with my daughter Nanny, who was about sixteen then. She is forty-one now, in the summer of 1996. That must have been twenty-five years ago now!

A ballerina, dancing on her toes, went *deedly-deedly-deedly* into the wings as she was supposed to do. But then there was a sound backstage as though she had put her foot in a bucket and then gone down an iron stairway with her foot still in the bucket.

I instantly laughed like hell.

I was the only person to do so.

A similar incident happened at a performance of the Indianapolis Symphony Orchestra when I was a kid. It didn't involve me, though, and it wasn't about laughter. There was this piece of music that was getting louder and louder, and was supposed to stop all of a sudden.

There was this woman in the same row with me, maybe ten seats away. She was talking to a friend during the crescendo, and she had to get louder and louder, too. The music stopped. She shrieked, "I FRY MINE IN BUTTER!"

31

My daughter Nanny and I went to Westminster Abbey the day after I became a pariah at the Royal Ballet. She was thunderstruck when she came face to face with the tomb of Sir Isaac Newton. At her age, and in that same place, my big brother Bernie, a born scientist who can't draw or paint for sour apples, would have shit an even bigger brick.

And well might any educated person excrete a sizable chunk of masonry when contemplating the tremendously truthful ideas this ordinary mortal, seemingly, uttered, with no more to go by, as far as we know, than signals from his dog's breakfast, from his three and a half pounds of blood-soaked sponge. This one naked ape invented differential calculus! He invented the reflecting telescope! He discovered and explained how a prism breaks a beam of sunlight into its constituent colors! He detected and wrote down previously unknown laws governing motion and gravity and optics!

Give us a break!

"Calling Dr. Fleon Sunoco! Sharpen your microtome. Do we ever have a *brain* for you!"

. . . . .

My daughter Nanny has a son, Max, who is twelve now, in 1996, halfway through the rerun. He will be seventeen when Kilgore Trout dies. This past April, Max wrote for school a really swell report on Sir Isaac Newton, a superman so ordinary in appearance. It told me something I hadn't known before: That Newton was advised by those who were his nominal supervisors to take time out from the hard truths of science to brush up on theology.

I like to think they did this not because they were foolish, but to remind him of how comforting and encouraging the make-believe of religion can be for common folk.

To quote from Kilgore Trout's story "Empire State," which is about a meteor the size and shape of the Manhattan skyscraper, approaching Earth point-first at a steady fifty-four miles an hour: "Science never cheered up anyone. The truth about the human situation is just too awful."

And the truth about that situation all over the world will never be worse than it was during the first couple of hours after the rerun stopped. Oh sure, there were millions of pedestrians lying on the ground because the weight on their feet had been unevenly distributed when free will kicked in. But most of them were pretty much OK, except for those who had been near the tops of escalators or stairways. Most were no worse hurt than the woman Allie and I saw come shooting out of a streetcar headfirst.

The real mayhem was wrought, as I said before, by self-propelled forms of transportation, of which there were none, of course, inside the former Museum of the American Indian. Things stayed peaceful in there, even as the crashing of vehicles and the cries of the injured and dying reached the climax of a crescendo outside.

"I fry mine in butter!" indeed.

The bums, or "sacred cattle," as Trout called them, had been seated or prone or supine when the timequake struck. That was how they were when the rerun ended. How could free will hurt them?

Trout would say of them afterward: "Even before the timequake, they had exhibited symptoms indistinguishable from those of PTA."

Only Trout jumped to his feet when a berserk fire truck, a hook-and-ladder, smacked the entrance of the Academy with its right front bumper and kept on going. What it did after that had nothing to do with people, and could have nothing to do with people. The sudden reduction of its velocity by its brush with the Academy caused the gaga firepersons aboard to hurtle through the air at the velocity it had reached going downhill from Broadway before it hit. Trout's best guess, based on how far the firepersons flew, was about fifty miles an hour.

Thus slowed and depopulated, the emergency vehicle made a sharp left turn into a cemetery across the street from the Academy. It started up a steep slope. It stopped short of the crest, and then rolled backward. The collision with the Academy had knocked its gearshift into *neutral*!

Momentum alone had carried it up the slope. The mighty motor roared. Its throttle was stuck. But the only opposition it could offer to gravity was the inertia of its own mass. It wasn't connected by the drive shaft to the back wheels anymore!

Listen to this: Gravity dragged the bellowing red monster back down into West 155th Street, and then ass-backward toward the Hudson River.

· · · · ·

The rescue vehicle's blow to the Academy was so severe, albeit glancing, that it caused a crystal chandelier to drop to the floor of the foyer.

The fancy light fixture missed the armed guard Dudley Prince by inches. If he hadn't been standing upright, his weight equally distributed between his feet when free will kicked in, he would have fallen prone in the direction he was facing, toward the front door. The chandelier would have *killed* him!

You want to talk about luck? When the timequake struck, Monica Pepper's paraplegic husband was ringing the doorbell. Dudley Prince was about to go to the steel front door. Before he could take a step in that direction, though, a smoke alarm went off in the picture gallery behind him. He froze. Which way to go?

So when free will kicked in, he was on the horns of the same dilemma. The smoke alarm behind him had saved his life!

When Trout learned of the miraculous escape from death by chandelier, thanks to a smoke alarm, he quoted Katharine Lee Bates, speaking rather than singing:

> *O beautiful for spacious skies,*
> *For amber waves of grain,*
> *For purple mountain majesties*
> *Above the fruited plain!*
> *America! America!*
> *God shed his grace on thee*
> *And crown thy good with brotherhood*
> *From sea to shining sea.*

The uniformed ex-convict, thanks to PTA, was a motivationally *kaput* statue when Kilgore Trout scampered in through the entrance, which was no longer blocked, minutes after the harsh rules of free will had been reinstated. Trout was shouting, "Wake up! For God's sake, wake up! Free will! Free will!"

Not only was the steel front door lying flat on the floor, bearing the enigmatic message "UCK AR," so Trout had to lope across it to reach Prince. It was still hinged and locked to the door frame. The door frame itself had let go on impact. It had parted from the surrounding masonry. The door and its hinges and bolts and *whoozit* were to all practical purposes as good as new, their frame had offered so little resistance to the berserk hook-and-ladder.

The contractor who installed the door and frame had cut corners when it came to securing the frame to the masonry. He had been a crook! As Trout would later say of him, and it might have been said of all corner-cutting contractors: "The wonder was that he could sleep at night!"

32

I say in speeches in 1996, halfway through the rerun to 2001, that I became a student in the Anthropology Department of the University of Chicago after World War Two. I say jokingly that I never should have studied that subject, because I can't stand primitive people. They're so *stupid*! The real reason my interest in the study of man as an animal flagged was that my wife Jane Marie Cox Vonnegut, who would die as Jane Marie Cox Yarmolinsky, gave birth to a baby named Mark. We needed bucks.

Jane herself, a Swarthmore Phi Beta Kappa, had won a full scholarship in the university's Russian Department. When she got pregnant with Mark, she resigned the scholarship. We found the head of the Russian Department in the library, I remember, and my wife told this melancholy refugee from Stalinism that she had to quit because she had become infected with progeny.

Even without a computer, I can never forget what he said to Jane: "My dear Mrs. Vonnegut, pregnancy is the *beginning*, not the end, of life."

. . . . .

The point I want to make, though, is that one course I took required me to read and then be ready to discuss *A Study of History* by the English historian Arnold Toynbee, who is up in Heaven now. He wrote about challenges and responses, saying that various civilizations persisted or failed depending on whether or not the challenges they faced were just too much for them. He gave examples.

The same might be said for individuals who would like to behave heroically, and most strikingly in the case of Kilgore Trout on the afternoon and evening of February 13th, 2001, after free will kicked in. If he had been in the area of Times Square, or near the entrance or exit of a major bridge or tunnel, or at an airport, where pilots, as they had learned to do during the rerun, had expected their planes to take off or land safely of their own accord, the challenge would have been too much not only for Trout but for anyone else.

What Trout beheld when he came out of the shelter in response to the crash next door was a horrifying scene all right, but the cast was small. The dead and dying were widely scattered, rather than heaped or enclosed in a burning or crumpled airplane or bus. They were still individuals. Alive or dead, they still had personalities, with stories to read in their faces and clothes.

Vehicular traffic on that stretch of West 155th Street, way-the-hell-and-gone uptown and leading nowhere, was at any time of day virtually nonexistent. This made the roaring hook-and-ladder a solo entertainer, as Trout watched gravity drag it ass-backward in the direction of the Hudson River. He was so free to think about the luckless fire truck in detail, despite the racket coming from busier thoroughfares, that he concluded calmly, as he would tell me at Xanadu, that one of three explanations for its helplessness had to be the right one: Either its gearshift was in reverse or neutral, or the drive shaft had snapped, or the clutch was shot.

He did not panic. His experiences as a forward observer for the artillery had taught him that panic only made things worse. He would say at Xanadu: "In real life, as in Grand Opera, arias only make hopeless situations worse."

True enough, he didn't panic. At the same time, though, he had yet to realize that he alone was ambulatory and wide awake. He had figured out the bare bones of what the Universe itself had done, contracted and then expanded. That was the *easy* part. What was actually happening, except for its actuality, might easily have been the ink-on-paper consequences of a premise for a story he himself had written and torn to pieces, and flushed down a toilet in a bus terminal or whatever, years ago.

Unlike Dudley Prince, Trout hadn't even earned a High School Equivalency Certificate, but he bore at least one surprising resemblance to my big brother Bernie, who has a Ph.D. in physical chemistry from MIT. Bernie and Trout had *both*, since their earliest adolescence, played games in their heads that began with this question: "If such-and-such were the case in our surroundings, what then, what then?"

What Trout had failed to extrapolate from the premise of the timequake and rerun, in the relative peace of the far end of West 155th Street, was that everybody for miles around was immobilized, if not by death or serious injury, then by PTA. He wasted precious minutes waiting for the arrival of healthy young ambulance crews and policepersons and more firepersons, and disaster specialists from the Red Cross and the Federal Emergency Management Agency, who would take care of things.

Please remember, for God's sake: He was eighty-fucking-four years old! Since he shaved every day, he was often mistaken for a bag lady rather than a bag gentleman, even without his baby-blanket babushka, and so incapable of inspiring any respect whatsoever. As for his sandals: At least they were tough. They were made of the same material as the brake shoes on the Apollo 11 spacecraft, which had delivered Neil Armstrong to the Moon, where he was the first human being ever to walk on it, in 1969.

The sandals were government surplus from the Vietnam War, the only war we ever lost, and during which Trout's only child Leon had been a deserter. American soldiers on patrol in that conflict wore the sandals over their lightweight jungle boots. They did that because the enemy used to stick spikes pointed upward, and dipped in shit so as to cause serious infections, in paths leading through the jungle.

Trout, so reluctant to play Russian roulette with free will again at his age, and especially with the lives of others at stake, finally realized that, for better or worse, he had better get his ass in gear. But what could he do?

33

My father often misquoted Shakespeare, but I never saw him read a book.

Yes, and I am here to suggest that the greatest writer in the English language so far was Lancelot Andrewes (1555–1626), and not the Bard of Avon (1564–1616). Poetry was certainly in the air back then. Try this:

> *The Lord is my shepherd; I shall not want.*
> *He maketh me to lie down in green pastures:*
> *he leadeth me beside the still waters.*
> *He restoreth my soul: he leadeth me in the paths of*
> *righteousness for his name's sake.*
> *Yea, though I walk through the valley of the shadow*
> *of death, I will fear no evil: for thou art with*
> *me; thy rod and thy staff they comfort me.*

Thou preparest a table before me in the presence of
mine enemies: thou anointest my head with
oil; my cup runneth over.
Surely goodness and mercy shall follow me all the
days of my life: and I will dwell in the
house of the Lord for ever.

Lancelot Andrewes was the chief translator and paraphraser among the scholars who gave us the King James Bible.

Did Kilgore Trout ever write poems? So far as I know, he wrote only one. He did it on the penultimate day of his life. He was fully aware that the Grim Reaper was coming, and coming soon. It is helpful to know that there is a tupelo tree between the mansion and the carriage house at Xanadu.

Wrote Trout:

When the tupelo
Goes poop-a-lo,
I'll come back to youp-a-lo.

34

My first wife Jane and my sister Allie had mothers who went nuts from time to time. Jane and Allie were graduates of Tudor Hall and had once been two of the prettiest, merriest girls at the Woodstock Golf and Country Club. All male writers, incidentally, no matter how broke or otherwise objectionable, have pretty wives. Somebody should look into this.

Jane and Allie missed the timequake, thank goodness. My guess is that Jane would have found some goodness in the rerun. Allie would not have. Jane was life-loving and optimistic, a scrapper against carcinoma to the very end. Allie's last words expressed relief, and nothing more. They were, as I've recorded elsewhere, "No pain, no pain." I didn't hear her say it, and neither did our big brother Bernie. A male hospital attendant, with a foreign accent, relayed those words to us via telephone.

I don't know what Jane's last words may have been. I've asked. She was Adam Yarmolinsky's wife by then, not mine. Jane evidently slipped away without speaking, not realizing that she wouldn't be coming up for air again. At her funeral, in an Episcopal church in Washington, D.C.,

Adam said to those gathered that her favorite exclamation was, "I can't wait!"

What Jane anticipated with such joy again and again was some event involving one or more of our six children, now all adults with children of their own: a psychiatric nurse, a comedy writer, a pediatrician, a painter, an airline pilot, and a printmaker.

I did not speak at her Episcopal obsequy. I wasn't up to it. Everything I had to say was for her ears alone, and she was gone. The last conversation we had, we two old friends from Indianapolis, was two weeks before she died. It was on the telephone. She was in Washington, D.C., where the Yarmolinskys had their home. I was in Manhattan, and married, as I still am, to the photographer and writer Jill Krementz.

I don't know which of us initiated the call, whose nickel it was. It could have been either one of us. Whoever it was, it turned out that the point of the call was to say good-bye.

Our son the doctor Mark would say after she died that he himself would never have submitted to all the medical procedures she acquiesced to in order to stay alive as long as she could, to go on saying, her eyes shining, "I can't wait!"

Our last conversation was intimate. Jane asked me, as though I knew, what would determine the exact moment of her death. She may have felt like a character in a book by me. In a sense she was. During our twenty-two years of marriage, I had decided where we were going next, to Chicago, to Schenectady, to Cape Cod. It was my work that determined what we did next. She never had a job. Raising six kids was enough for her.

I told her on the telephone that a sunburned, raffish, bored but not unhappy ten-year-old boy, whom we did not know, would be standing on the gravel slope of the boat-launching ramp at the foot of Scudder's Lane. He would gaze out at nothing in particular, birds, boats, or whatever, in the harbor of Barnstable, Cape Cod.

At the head of Scudder's Lane, on Route 6A, one-tenth of a mile from the boat-launching ramp, is the big old house where we cared for our son and two daughters and three sons of my sister's until they were grownups. Our daughter Edith and her builder husband, John Squibb, and their small sons, Will and Buck, live there now.

I told Jane that this boy, with nothing better to do, would pick up a stone, as boys will. He would arc it over the harbor. When the stone hit the water, she would die.

Jane could believe with all her heart anything that made being alive seem full of white magic. That was her strength. She was raised a Quaker, but stopped going to meetings of Friends after her four happy years at Swarthmore. She became an Episcopalian after marrying Adam, who remained a Jew. She died believing in the Trinity and Heaven and Hell and all the rest of it. I'm so glad. Why? Because I loved her.

35

Tellers of stories with ink on paper, not that they matter anymore, have been either *swoopers* or *bashers*. Swoopers write a story quickly, higgledy-piggledy, crinkum-crankum, any which way. Then they go over it again painstakingly, fixing everything that is just plain awful or doesn't work. Bashers go one sentence at a time, getting it exactly right before they go on to the next one. When they're done they're done.

I am a basher. Most men are bashers, and most women are swoopers. Again: Somebody should look into this. It may be that writers of either sex are *born* to be swoopers or bashers. I visited Rockefeller University recently, and they are seeking and finding more and more genes that tend to *make us* behave this way or that way, just as a rerun after a timequake would do. Even before that visit, it had appeared to me that Jane's and my children and Allie's and Jim's children, while not alike as grownups, had each become the sort of grownups they practically *had to be.*

All six are OK.

Then again, all six have had countless opportunities to be OK. If you can believe what you read in the papers, or what you hear and see on TV and the Information Superhighway, most people don't.

Writers who are swoopers, it seems to me, find it wonderful that people are funny or tragic or whatever, *worth reporting*, without wondering why or how people are alive in the first place.

Bashers, while ostensibly making sentence after sentence as efficient as possible, may actually be breaking down seeming doors and fences, cutting their ways through seeming barbed-wire entanglements, under fire and in an atmosphere of mustard gas, in search of answers to these eternal questions: "What in heck should we be doing? What in heck is really going on?"

If bashers are unwilling to settle for the basher Voltaire's *"Il faut cultiver notre jardin,"* that leaves the politics of human rights, which I am prepared to discuss. I begin with a couple of true stories from the end of Trout's and my war in Europe.

Here's the thing: For a few days after Germany surrendered, on May 7th, 1945, having been directly or indirectly responsible for the deaths of maybe forty million people, there was a pocket of anarchy south of Dresden, near the Czech border, which had yet to be occupied and policed by troops of the Soviet Union. I was in it, and have described it some in my novel *Bluebeard*. Thousands of prisoners of war like myself had been turned loose there, along with death camp survivors with tattooed arms, and lunatics and convicted felons and Gypsies, and who knows what else.

Get this: There were also German troops there, still armed but humbled, and looking for anybody but the Soviet Union to surrender to. My particular war buddy Bernard V. O'Hare and I talked to some of them.

119

O'Hare, having become a lawyer for both the prosecution and the defense in later life, is up in Heaven now. Back then, though, we could both hear the Germans saying that America would now have to do what they had been doing, which was to fight the godless Communists.

We replied that we didn't think so. We expected the USSR to try to become more like the USA, with freedom of speech and religion, and fair trials and honestly elected officials, and so on. We, in turn, would try to do what they claimed to be doing, which was to distribute goods and services and opportunities more fairly: "From each according to his abilities, to each according to his needs." That sort of thing.

Occam's Razor.

And then O'Hare and I, not much more than kids actually, went into an undefended barn there in the springtime countryside. We wanted something to eat, anything to eat. But we found a wounded and obviously dying captain of the notoriously heartless Nazi Schutzstaffel, the SS, in a haymow instead. He might easily, until very recently, have been in charge of tormenting and planning the extinction of some of the death camp survivors not far away.

Like all members of the SS, and like all death camp survivors as well, this captain presumably had a serial number tattooed on his arm. Want to talk about postwar *irony*? There was a lot of that.

He asked O'Hare and me to go away. He would soon be dead, and said he looked forward to being such. As we prepared to depart, not feeling much about him one way or the other, he cleared his throat, signaling that he had something more to say after all. This was the last-words business again. If he had any, who but us could hear them?

"I have just wasted the past ten years of my life," he said.

You want to talk about a timequake?

36

My wife thinks I think I'm such hot stuff. She's wrong. I don't think I'm such hot stuff.

My hero George Bernard Shaw, socialist, and shrewd and funny playwright, said in his eighties that if he was considered smart, he sure pitied people who were considered dumb. He said that, having lived as long as he had, he was at last sufficiently wise to serve as a reasonably competent office boy.

That's how *I* feel.

When the City of London wanted to give Shaw its Order of Merit, he thanked them for it, but said he had already given it to himself.

I would have accepted it. I would have recognized the opportunity for a world-class joke, but would never allow myself to be funny at the cost of making somebody else feel like something the cat drug in.

Let that be my epitaph.

· · · · ·

In the waning summer of 1996, I ask myself if there were ideas I once held that I should now repudiate. I consider the example set by my father's only brother, Uncle Alex, the childless, Harvard-educated Indianapolis insurance salesman. He had me reading high-level socialist writers like Shaw and Norman Thomas and Eugene Debs and John Dos Passos when I was a teenager, along with making model airplanes and jerking off. After World War Two, Uncle Alex became as politically conservative as the Archangel Gabriel.

But I still like what O'Hare and I said to German soldiers right after we were liberated: That America was going to become more socialist, was going to try harder to give everybody work to do, and to ensure that our children, at least, weren't hungry or cold or illiterate or scared to death.

Lotsa luck!

I still quote Eugene Debs (1855–1926), late of Terre Haute, Indiana, five times the Socialist Party's candidate for President, in every speech:

"While there is a lower class I am in it, while there is a criminal element I am of it; while there is a soul in prison, I am not free."

In recent years, I've found it prudent to say before quoting Debs that he is to be taken *seriously.* Otherwise many in the audience will start to laugh. They are being nice, not mean, knowing I like to be funny. But it is also a sign of these times that such a moving echo of the Sermon on the Mount can be perceived as outdated, wholly discredited horsecrap.

Which it is not.

37

Kilgore Trout's rugged jungle sandals crunched on crystal fragments from the fallen chandelier as he loped across the face of the fallen steel front door and frame, which said "UCK AR." Since there were crystal shards atop the door and frame instead of underneath them, a forensic scientist would have had to testify in a lawsuit, if one had ever been filed against the crooked contractor, that the crook's handiwork fell first. The chandelier must have dangled for a second or so before letting gravity do to it what gravity apparently would have liked to do to simply *everything*.

The smoke alarm in the picture gallery was still ringing, "presumably," Trout would later say, "continuing to do so of its own free will." He was joking, making fun, as was his wont, of the idea that there had ever been free will for anyone or anything, rerun or not.

The Academy doorbell had clammed up the moment Zoltan Pepper was hit by the fire truck. Trout's words again: "Quoth the doorbell with its silence, 'No comment at this time.' "

Trout himself, as I've said, was nevertheless espousing free will when he entered the Academy, and was invoking the Judeo-Christian deity as well: "Wake up! For God's sake, wake up, wake up! Free will! Free will!"

He would say at Xanadu that even if he had been a hero that afternoon and night, his entering the Academy, "pretending," in his words, "to be Paul Revere in the space-time continuum," had been "an act of sheer cowardice."

He was seeking shelter from the growing din on Broadway, half a block away, and from the sounds of really serious explosions from other parts of the city. A mile and a half to the south, near Grant's Tomb, a massive Department of Sanitation truck, for want of sincere steering, plowed through the lobby of a condominium and into the apartment of the building superintendent. It knocked over his gas range. The ruptured pipe of that major appliance filled the stairwell and elevator shaft of the six-story structure with methane laced with skunk smell. Most of the tenants were on Social Security.

And then KA-BOOM!

"An accident waiting to happen," as Kilgore Trout would say at Xanadu.

The old science fiction writer wanted to galvanize the armed and uniformed Dudley Prince into action, he later confessed, so that he himself wouldn't have to do anything more. "Free will! Free will! Fire! Fire!" he shouted at Prince.

Prince did not move a muscle. He batted his eyes, but those were reflexes, and not free will, like me and the chicken noodle soup. One thing Prince was thinking, by his own account, was that if he moved a muscle, he might find himself in the New York State Maximum Security Adult Correctional Facility at Athena back in 1991 again.

Understandable!

So Trout bypassed Prince for the moment, confessedly still looking out for *numero uno*. A smoke alarm was raising hell. If the building was really on fire, and the fire could not be brought under control, then Trout was going to have to find someplace else where a senior citizen could hunker down until whatever was going on outside died down some.

He found a lit cigar resting on a saucer in the picture gallery. The cigar, although illegal everywhere in New York County, was not yet, and probably never would be, a danger to anyone but itself. Its midpoint was centered in the saucer, so it wasn't going anywhere else as it oxidized. But the smoke alarm was yelling about the end of civilization as we had known it.

Trout, in *My Ten Years on Automatic Pilot*, would synthesize what he should have said to the smoke alarm that afternoon: "Nonsense! Get a grip on yourself, you brainless nervous breakdown."

Here's the spooky part: There wasn't anybody but Trout in the gallery!

Could it be that the American Academy of Arts and Letters was haunted by *poltergeists*?

38

I got a good letter today, Friday, August 23rd, 1996, from a young stranger named Jeff Mihalich, one would guess of Serb or Croat descent, who is majoring in physics at the University of Illinois at Urbana. Jeff says he enjoyed his physics course in high school, and got top grades, but "ever since I have had physics at the university I have had much trouble with it. This was a huge blow to me because I was used to doing well in school. I thought there was nothing I couldn't do if I just wanted it bad enough."

My reply will go like this: "You might want to read the picaresque novel *The Adventures of Augie March* by Saul Bellow. The epiphany at the end, as I recall, is that we shouldn't be seeking harrowing challenges, but rather tasks we find natural and interesting, tasks we were apparently born to perform.

"As for the charms of physics: Two of the most entertaining subjects taught in high school or college are *mechanics* and *optics*. Beyond these playful disciplines, however, lie mind games as dependent on native talent as playing the French horn or chess.

"Of native talent itself I say in speeches: 'If you go to a big city, and a university is a big city, you are bound to run into Wolfgang Amadeus Mozart. Stay home, stay home.' "

To put it another way: No matter what a young person thinks he or she is really hot stuff at doing, he or she is sooner or later going to run into somebody in the same field who will cut him or her a new asshole, so to speak.

A boyhood friend of mine, William H. C. "Skip" Failey, who died four months ago and is up in Heaven now, had good reason when a high school sophomore to think of himself as unbeatable at Ping-Pong. I am no slouch at Ping-Pong myself, but I wouldn't play against Skip. He put so much spin on his serve that no matter how I tried to return it, I already knew it would go up my nose or out the window or back to the factory, anywhere but on the table.

When Skip was a junior, though, he played a classmate of ours, Roger Downs. Skip said afterward, "Roger cut me a new asshole."

Thirty-five years after that, I was lecturing at a university in Colorado, and who should be in the audience but Roger Downs! Roger had become a businessperson out that way, and a respected competitor on the Senior Men's Tennis Circuit. So I congratulated him on having given Skip a table tennis lesson so long ago.

Roger was eager to hear anything Skip might have said after that showdown. I said, "Skip said you cut him a new asshole."

Roger was enormously satisfied, as well he might have been.

I did not ask, but the surgical metaphor could not have been unfamiliar to him. Furthermore, life being the Darwinian experiment, or "crock of shit," as Trout liked to call it, Roger himself had surely departed more than one tennis tournament having, like Skip, undergone a colostomy to his self-regard.

. . . . .

More news of this day in August, halfway through the rerun, as yet another autumn draws near: My big brother Bernie, the born scientist who may know more about the electrification of thunderstorms than anyone, has an invariably fatal cancer, too far advanced to be daunted by the Three Horsemen of the Oncologic Apocalypse, Surgery, Chemotherapy, and Radiation.

Bernie still feels fine.

It is much too early to talk about, but when he dies, God forbid, I don't think his ashes should be put in Crown Hill Cemetery with James Whitcomb Riley and John Dillinger, who belonged only to Indiana. Bernie belongs to the World.

Bernie's ashes should be scattered over the dome of a towering thunderhead.

39

So there was Roger Downs of Indianapolis in Colorado. Here am I, of Indianapolis, on the South Fork of Long Island. The ashes of my Indianapolis wife Jane Marie Cox are mixed with the roots of a flowering cherry tree, unmarked, in Barnstable Village, Massachusetts. The branches of that tree can be seen from the ell that Ted Adler rebuilt from scratch, after which he asked, "How the hell did I *do* that?"

The Best Man at Jane's and my wedding in Indianapolis, Benjamin Hitz of Indianapolis, is a widower now in Santa Barbara, California. Ben dated an Indianapolis cousin of mine several times this spring. She is a widow on the seacoast of Maryland, and my sister died in New Jersey, and my brother, although he doesn't feel like it yet, is dying in Albany, New York.

My boyhood pal David Craig, who made a radio in a German tank stop playing popular music during World War Two, is a builder in New Orleans. My cousin Emmy, whose dad told me I was a man at last when I came home from war, and who was my lab partner in physics class at

Shortridge High School, lives only about thirty miles east of Dave in Louisiana.

Diaspora!

Why did so many of us bug out of a city built by our ancestors, where our family names were respected, whose streets and speech were so familiar, and where, as I said at Butler University last June, there was indeed the best and worst of Western Civilization?

Adventure!

It may be, too, that we wanted to escape the powerful pull, not of gravity, which is everywhere, but of Crown Hill Cemetery.

Crown Hill got my sister Allie. It didn't get Jane. It won't get my big brother Bernie. It won't get me.

I lectured in 1990 at a university in southern Ohio. They put me up in a motel nearby. When I returned to the motel after my speech, and was having my customary scotch and soda so I would sleep like a baby, which is the way I like to sleep, the bar was congenially populated by obviously local old people who seemed to really like each other. They had a lot to laugh about. They were all comedians.

I asked the bartender who they were. He said they were the fiftieth reunion of the Class of 1940 of Zanesville High School. It sure looked nice. It sure looked right. I was in the Class of 1940 at Shortridge High School, and was then skipping my own reunion.

Those people might have been characters out of *Our Town* by Thornton Wilder, as sweet a play as can ever be.

. . . . .

They and I were so old that we could remember when it didn't matter all that much economically whether you did or didn't go to college. You could still amount to something. And I told my father back then that maybe I didn't want to become a chemist like my big brother Bernie. I could save him a ton of money if I went to work for a newspaper instead.

Understand: I could go to college only if I took the same sorts of courses my brother had. Father and Bernie were agreed on that. Any other sort of higher education was what they both called *ornamental*. They laughed at Uncle Alex the insurance salesman because his education at Harvard had been so *ornamental*.

Father said I had better talk to his close friend Fred Bates Johnson, a lawyer who as a young man had been a reporter for the now defunct Democratic daily *The Indianapolis Times*.

I knew Mr. Johnson pretty well. Father and I used to go hunting for rabbits and birds with him down in Brown County, before Allie cried so much we had to give it up. He asked me there in his office, leaning back in his swivel chair, his eyes slits, how I planned to begin my career as a journalist.

"Well, sir," I said, "I thought maybe I could get a job on *The Culver Citizen* and work there for three or four years. I know the area pretty well." Culver was on Lake Maxincuckee in northern Indiana. We used to have a summer cottage on that lake.

"And then?" he said.

"With that much experience," I said, "I should be able to get a job with a much bigger paper, maybe in Richmond or Kokomo."

"And then?" he said.

"After maybe five years on a paper like that," I said, "I think I'd be ready to take a shot at Indianapolis."

"You'll have to excuse me," he said, "but I have to make a phone call."

"Of course," I said.

He swiveled around so his back was to me when he made the call. He spoke softly, but I wasn't trying to overhear. I figured it was none of my business.

He hung up the phone and swiveled around to face me again. "Congratulations!" he said. "You have a job on *The Indianapolis Times*."

40

I went to college in faraway Ithaca, New York, instead of going to work for *The Indianapolis Times*. Ever since, I, like Blanche DuBois in *A Streetcar Named Desire*, have always depended on the kindness of strangers.

I think now, with the clambake at Xanadu only five years away, about a man I might have been, spending his adult life among those he went to high school with, loving and hating, as had his parents and grandparents, a town that was his own.

He's gone!

> *Full fathom five he lies;*
>   *Of his bones are coral made:*
> *Those are pearls that were his eyes:*
>   *Nothing of him that doth fade,*

But doth suffer a sea-change
Into something rich and strange.

He would have known several jokes I know, like the one Fred Bates Johnson told one time, when he and Father and I, just a kid, and some others, were hunting down in Brown County. According to Fred, a bunch of guys like us went hunting for deer and moose up in Canada. Somebody had to do the cooking, or they would all starve to death.

They drew straws to see who would cook while the others hunted from dawn to dusk. To make the joke more immediate, Fred said it was Father who got the short straw. Father could cook. Mother couldn't. She was proud she couldn't cook, and wouldn't wash dishes and so on. I liked to go over to other kids' houses, where their mothers did those things.

The hunters agreed that anybody who complained about Father's cooking became the cook. So Father prepared worse and worse meals, while the others were having one hell of a good time in the forest. No matter how awful a supper was, though, the hunters pronounced it lip-smacking delicious, clapping Father on the back and so on.

After they marched off one morning, Father found a pile of fresh moose poop outside. He fried it in motor oil. That night he served it as steaming patties.

The first guy to taste one spit it out. He couldn't *help* himself! He spluttered, "Jesus Christ! That tastes like moose poop fried in motor oil!"

But then he added, "But *good*, but *good*!"

. . . . .

I think Mother was raised to be so useless because her father Albert Lieber, the brewer and speculator, believed that America was going to have an aristocracy based on the European model. Proofs of membership in such a caste over there, and so it would be over here, too, he must have reasoned, were wives and daughters who were ornamental.

41

I don't think I missed the boat when I failed to write a novel about Albert Lieber, and how he was largely responsible for my mother's suicide on Mother's Day Eve, 1944. German-Americans in Indianapolis lack universality. They have never been sympathetically, or even villainously, stereotyped in movies or books or plays. I would have had to explain them from scratch.

Lotsa luck!

The great critic H. L. Mencken, himself a German-American, but living all his life in Baltimore, Maryland, confessed that he had difficulty in concentrating on the novels of Willa Cather. Try as he might, he couldn't really care a whole lot about Czech immigrants in Nebraska.

Same problem.

I will say for the record that my grandfather Albert Lieber's first wife, Alice, née Barus, namesake of my sister Allie, died giving birth to her third child, who was Uncle Rudy. Mother was her first. The middle child was Uncle Pete, who flunked out of MIT, but who nonetheless sired a nuclear scientist, my cousin Albert in Del Mar, California. Cousin Albert reports that he has just gone blind.

It isn't radiation that has made cousin Albert blind. It is something else, which could have happened to anybody, in or out of science. Cousin Albert himself has sired a non-nuclear-type scientist, a computer whiz.

As Kilgore Trout used to exclaim from time to time, "Life goes on!"

The point I want to make is that Mother's father, the brewer, Republican big shot, and neo-aristocratic bon vivant, married a violinist after his first wife died. She turned out to be clinically bughouse. Face it! Some women are! She hated his kids with a passion. She was jealous of his love for them. She wanted to be the whole show. Some women do!

This female bat out of hell, who could play a fiddle like nobody's business, abused Mother and Uncle Pete and Uncle Rudy so ferociously, both physically and mentally, during their formative years, before Grandfather Lieber divorced her, that they never got over it.

If there had been a significant body of potential book-buyers who might care about rich German-Americans in Indianapolis, it would have been a piece of cake for me to bang out a roman-fleuve demonstrating that my grandfather in fact *murdered* my mother, albeit very slowly, by double-crossing her so long ago.

"Ting-a-ling, you son of a bitch!"

Working title: *Gone With the Wind.*

When Mother married my father, a young architect in moderate circumstances, politicians and saloonkeepers and the cream of Indianapolis German-American society gave them a treasure trove of crystal and linens and china and silver, and even some gold.

Scheherazade!

Who could doubt then that even Indiana had its own hereditary aristocracy, with useless possessions to rival those of horses' asses in the other hemisphere?

It all seemed like a lot of junk to my brother and my sister and our father and me during the Great Depression. It is now as widely dispersed as the Class of 1940 of Shortridge High School.

Auf Wiedersehen.

42

I always had trouble ending short stories in ways that would satisfy a general public. In real life, as during a rerun following a timequake, people don't change, don't learn anything from their mistakes, and don't apologize. In a short story they have to do at least two out of three of those things, or you might as well throw it away in the lidless wire trash receptacle chained and padlocked to the fire hydrant in front of the American Academy of Arts and Letters.

OK, I could handle that. But after I had a character change and/or learn something and/or apologize, that left the cast standing around with their thumbs up their asses. That is no way to tell a reader the show is over.

In my salad days, when I was green in judgment, and never having asked to be born in the first place, I sought the advice of my then literary agent as to how to end stories without killing all the characters. He had been fiction editor of an important magazine, and a story consultant for a Hollywood studio as well.

He said, "Nothing could be simpler, dear boy: The hero mounts his horse and rides off into the sunset."

Many years later, he would kill himself on purpose with a twelve-gauge shotgun.

Another friend and client of his said he couldn't possibly have committed suicide, it was so *out of character.*

I replied, "Even with military training, there is no way a man can accidentally blow his head off with a shotgun."

Many years earlier, so long ago that I was a student at the University of Chicago, I had a conversation with my thesis advisor about the arts in general. At that time, I had no idea that I personally would go into any sort of art.

He said, "You know what artists are?"

I didn't.

"Artists," he said, "are people who say, 'I can't fix my country or my state or my city, or even my marriage. But by golly, I can make this square of canvas, or this eight-and-a-half-by-eleven piece of paper, or this lump of clay, or these twelve bars of music, exactly what they *ought* to be!'"

About five years after that, he did what Hitler's Minister of Propaganda and his wife and their kids did at the end of World War Two. He swallowed potassium cyanide.

I wrote a letter to his widow, saying how much his teachings had meant to me. I did not get an answer. It could be that she was overwhelmed with grief. Then again, she may have been sore as hell at him for taking the easy way out.

140

. . . . .

This very summer, I asked the novelist William Styron in a Chinese restaurant how many people on the whole planet had what we had, which was lives worth living. Between the two of us, we came up with *seventeen percent*.

The next day I took a walk in midtown Manhattan with a longtime friend, a physician who treats every sort of addict at Bellevue Hospital. Many of his patients are homeless and HIV-positive as well. I told him about Styron's and my figure of seventeen percent. He said it sounded about right to him.

As I have written elsewhere, this man is a saint. I define a saint as a person who behaves decently in an indecent society.

I asked him why half his patients at Bellevue didn't commit suicide. He said the same question had occurred to him. He sometimes asked them, as though it were an unremarkable part of a diagnostic routine, if they had thoughts of self-destruction. He said that they were almost without exception surprised and insulted by the question. An idea *that sick* had never entered their heads!

It was about then that we passed an ex-patient of his who was toting a plastic bag filled with aluminum cans he had gathered. He was one of Kilgore Trout's "sacred cattle," somehow wonderful despite his economic uselessness.

"Hi, Doc," he said.

43

Question: What is the white stuff in bird poop?
Answer: That is bird poop, too.

So much for science, and how helpful it can be in these times of environmental calamities. Chernobyl is still hotter than a Hiroshima baby carriage. Our underarm deodorants have eaten holes in the ozone layer.

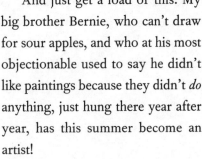

Art or not?

And just get a load of this: My big brother Bernie, who can't draw for sour apples, and who at his most objectionable used to say he didn't like paintings because they didn't *do* anything, just hung there year after year, has this summer become an artist!

I shit you not! This Ph.D. physical chemist from MIT is now the poor man's Jackson Pollock! He squoozles glurp of various colors and consistencies between two flat sheets of impermeable materials, such as windowpanes or bathroom tiles. He pulls them apart, *et voilà!* This has nothing to do with his cancer. He didn't know he had it yet, and the malignancy was in his lungs and not his brain in any case. He was just farting around one day, a semi-retired old geezer without a wife to ask him what in the name of God he thought he was doing, *et voilà!* Better late than never, that's all I can say.

So he sent me some black-and-white Xeroxes of his squiggly miniatures, mostly dendritic forms, maybe trees or shrubs, maybe mushrooms or umbrellas full of holes, but really quite interesting. Like my ballroom dancing, they were *acceptable.* He has since sent me multicolored originals, which I like a lot.

The message he sent me along with the Xeroxes, though, wasn't about unexpected happiness. It was an unreconstructed technocrat's challenge to the artsy-fartsy, of which I was a prime exemplar. "Is this art or not?" he asked. He couldn't have put that question so jeeringly fifty years ago, of course, before the founding of the first wholly American school of painting, Abstract Expressionism, and the deification in particular of Jack the Dripper, Jackson Pollock, who also couldn't draw for sour apples.

Bernie said, too, that a very interesting *scientific phenomenon* was involved, having to do, he left me to guess, with how different glurps behave when squoozled this way and that, with nowhere to go but up or down or sideways. If the artsy-fartsy world had no use for his pictures, he seemed to imply, his pictures could still point the way to better lubricants or suntan lotions, or who knows what? The all-new Preparation H!

He would not sign his pictures, he said, or admit publicly that he had made them, or describe how they were made. He plainly expected puffed-up critics to sweat bullets and excrete sizable chunks of masonry when trying to answer his cunningly innocent question: "Art or not?"

I was pleased to reply with an epistle which was frankly vengeful, since he and Father had screwed me out of a liberal arts college education: "Dear Brother: This is almost like telling you about the birds and the bees," I began. "There are many good people who are beneficially stimulated by some, but not all, manmade arrangements of colors and shapes on flat surfaces, essentially *nonsense*.

"You yourself are gratified by some music, arrangements of noises, and again essentially *nonsense*. If I were to kick a bucket down the cellar stairs, and then say to you that the racket I had made was philosophically on a par with *The Magic Flute,* this would not be the beginning of a long and upsetting debate. An utterly satisfactory and complete response on your part would be, 'I like what Mozart did, and I hate what the bucket did.'

"Contemplating a purported work of art is a social activity. Either you have a rewarding time, or you don't. You don't have to say *why* afterward. You don't have to say anything.

"You are a justly revered experimentalist, dear Brother. If you really want to know whether your pictures are, as you say, 'art or not,' you must display them in a public place somewhere, and see if strangers like to look at them. That is the way the game is played. Let me know what happens."

I went on: "People capable of liking some paintings or prints or whatever can rarely do so without knowing something about the artist. Again, the situation is social rather than scientific. Any work of art is half of a conversation between two human beings, and it helps a lot to know who is talking at you. Does he or she have a reputation for seriousness, for religiosity, for suffering, for concupiscence, for rebellion, for sincerity, for jokes?

"There are virtually no respected paintings made by persons about whom we know zilch. We can even surmise quite a bit about the lives of whoever did the paintings in the caverns underneath Lascaux, France.

"I dare to suggest that no picture can attract serious attention without a particular sort of human being attached to it in the viewer's mind. If you are unwilling to claim credit for your pictures, and to say why you hoped others might find them worth examining, there goes the ball game.

"Pictures are famous for their humanness, and not for their pictureness."

I went on: "There is also the matter of craftsmanship. Real picture-lovers like to *play along,* so to speak, to look closely at the surfaces, to see how the illusion was created. If you are unwilling to say how you made your pictures, there goes the ball game a second time.

"Good luck, and love as always," I wrote. And I signed my name.

44

I myself paint pictures on sheets of acetate with black India ink. An artist half my age, Joe Petro III, who lives and works in Lexington, Kentucky, prints them by means of the silk-screen process. I paint a separate acetate sheet, again in opaque black, for each color I want Joe to use. I do not see my pictures, which I have painted in black alone, in color until Joe has printed them, one color at a time.

I make negatives for his positives.

There may be easier, quicker, and cheaper ways to create pictures. They might leave us more time for golf, and for making model airplanes and whacking off. We should look into that. Joe's studio looks like something out of the Middle Ages.

I can't thank Joe enough for having me make negatives for his positives after the little radio in my head stopped receiving messages from wherever it is the bright ideas come from. Art is so *absorbing*.

It is a *sopper-upper.*

. . . . .

Listen: Only three weeks ago at this writing, on September 6th, 1996, Joe and I opened a show of twenty-six of our prints in the 1/1 Gallery in Denver, Colorado. A local microbrewery, Wynkoop, bottled a special beer for the occasion. The label was one of my self-portraits. The name of the beer was Kurt's Mile-High Malt.

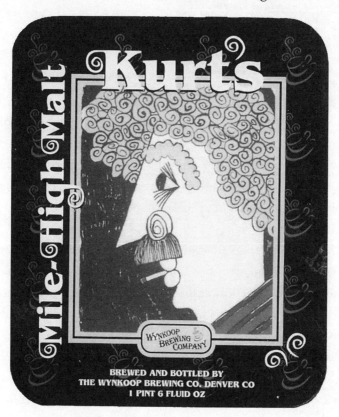

You think that wasn't fun? Try this: The beer, at my suggestion, was lightly flavored with coffee. What was so great about that? It tasted really good, for one thing, but it was also an homage to my maternal grandfather

Albert Lieber, who was a brewer until he was put out of business by Prohibition in 1920. The secret ingredient in the beer that won a Gold Medal for the Indianapolis Brewery at the Paris Exposition of 1889 was coffee!

Ting-a-ling!

That still wasn't enough fun out there in Denver? OK, how about the fact that the name of the owner of the Wynkoop Brewing Company, a guy about Joe's age, was John Hickenlooper? So what? Only this: When I went to Cornell University to become a chemist fifty-six years ago, I was made a fraternity brother of a man named John Hickenlooper.

Ting-a-ling?

This was his son! My fraternity brother had died when this son was only seven. I knew more about him than his own son did! I was able to tell this young Denver brewer that his dad, in partnership with another Delta Upsilon brother, John Locke, sold candy and soft drinks and cigarettes out of a big closet at the top of the stairs on the second floor of the fraternity house.

They christened it *Hickenlooper's Lockenbar*. We called it *Lockenlooper's Hickenbar*, and *Barkenhicker's Loopenlock*, and *Lockenbarker's Loopenhick*, and so on.

Happy days! We thought we'd live forever.

Old beer in new bottles. Old jokes in new people.

. . . . .

I told young John Hickenlooper a joke his dad taught me. It worked like this: His dad would say to me, no matter where we were, "Are you a member of the Turtle Club?" I had no choice but to bellow at the top of my lungs, "YOU BET YOUR ASS I AM!"

I could do the same thing to his dad. On some particularly solemn and sacred occasion, such as the swearing in of new fraternity brothers, I might whisper to him, "Are you a member of the Turtle Club?" He would have no choice but to bellow at the top of his lungs, "YOU BET YOUR ASS I AM!"

45

Another old joke: "Hello, my name is Spalding. No doubt you've played with my balls." It doesn't work anymore because Spalding is no longer a major manufacturer of athletic equipment, just as Lieber Gold Medal Beer is no longer a popular recreational drug in the Middle West, and just as the Vonnegut Hardware Company is no longer a manufacturer and retailer of durable and eminently practical goods out that way.

The hardware company was put out of business fair and square by livelier competitors. The Indianapolis Brewery was shut down by Article XVIII of the United States Constitution, which declared in 1919 that the manufacture, sale, or transportation of intoxicating liquors was against the law.

The Indianapolis humorist Kin Hubbard said about Prohibition that it was "better than no liquor at all." Intoxicating liquors did not become lawful again until 1933. By then, the bootlegger Al Capone owned Chicago, and Joseph P. Kennedy, father of a murdered-President-to-be, was a multimillionaire.

· · · · ·

At the daybreak that followed the opening of Joe Petro III's and my show in Denver, a Sunday, I awoke alone in a room in the oldest hotel there, the Oxford. I knew where I was and how I had gotten there. It wasn't as though I had been drunk as a hooty-owl on Grandfather's beer the night before.

I dressed and stepped outside. Nobody else I could see was up yet. There were no moving vehicles. If free will had chosen to kick in again at that moment, and I had been off balance and so fallen down, nobody would have run over me.

The best thing to be when free will kicks in, probably, is a Mbuti, a Pygmy in a rain forest in Zaire, Africa.

Two hundred yards from my hotel was the husk of what used to be the throbbing heart of the city, its turgid auricles and ventricles. I mean its passenger railroad station. It was completed in 1880. Only two trains a day stop there now.

I myself was antique enough to remember as terrific music the hissing and rolling thunder of steam locomotives, and their mournful whistles, and the metronomic clicks of wheels on joints in the rails, and the apparent rise and fall, thanks to the Doppler effect, of the pitch of warning bells at crossings.

I remembered labor history, too, because the first effective strikes by American working people for better pay, and more respect, and safer working conditions, were called against the railroads. And then against owners of coal mines and steel mills and textile mills, and on and on. Much blood was shed in what appeared to most members of my generation of American writers to be battles as worth fighting as any against a foreign enemy.

The optimism that infused so much of our writing was based on our belief that after Magna Carta, and then the Declaration of Independence, and then the Bill of Rights, and then the Emancipation Proclamation, and then Article XIX of the Constitution, which in 1920 entitled women to vote, some scheme for economic justice could also be devised. That was the logical next step.

And even in 1996, I in speeches propose the following amendments to the Constitution:

Article XXVIII: Every newborn shall be sincerely welcomed and cared for until maturity.

Article XXIX: Every adult who needs it shall be given meaningful work to do, at a living wage.

What we have created instead, as customers and employees and investors, is mountains of paper wealth so enormous that a handful of people in charge of them can take millions and billions for themselves without hurting anyone. Apparently.

Many members of my generation are disappointed.

46

Can you believe it? Kilgore Trout, who never even saw a stage play until he got to Xanadu, not only wrote a play after he got home from our war, which was World War Two, but he *copyrighted* it! I have just retrieved it from the memory banks of the Library of Congress, and it is entitled *The Wrinkled Old Family Retainer.*

It is like a birthday present from my computer here in the Sinclair Lewis Suite at Xanadu. Wow! The date yesterday was November 11th, 2010. I have just turned eighty-eight, or ninety-eight, if you want to count the rerun. My wife, Monica Pepper Vonnegut, says eighty-eight is a very lucky number, and so is ninety-eight. She is heavily into numerology.

My darling daughter Lily will turn twenty-eight on December 15th! Who ever thought I would live to see that day?

The Wrinkled Old Family Retainer is about a wedding. The bride is *Mirabile Dictu,* a virgin. The groom is *Flagrante Delicto,* a heartless womanizer.

Sotto Voce, a male guest standing at the fringe of the ceremony, says out of the corner of his mouth to a guy standing next to him, "I don't bother with all this. I simply find a woman who hates me, and I give her a house."

And the other guy says, as the groom is kissing the bride, "All women are psychotic. All men are jerks."

The eponymous wrinkled old family retainer, crying his rheumy eyes out behind a potted palm, is *Scrotum.*

Monica is still obsessed by the mystery of who left a cigar smoldering beneath the smoke alarm in the picture gallery of the Academy minutes before free will kicked in again. That was more than nine years ago! Who cares? What difference can knowing that make? That's like knowing what the white stuff in bird poop is.

What Kilgore Trout did with that cigar was scrooch it out in the saucer. He scrooched and scrooched and scrooched it, by his own admission to Monica and me, as though it were responsible not only for the yelling of the smoke alarm, but for all the din outside as well.

"The wheel that squeaks the loudest gets the oil," he said.

He realized the absurdity of what he was doing, he said, only when, as he took a painting down from the wall, preparing to hit the alarm with a corner of the frame, the alarm fell silent of its own accord.

He hung up the painting again, and even made sure it was hanging straight. "That seemed somehow important, that the picture was nice and straight," he said, "and evenly spaced from the others. At least I could make that little part of the chaotic Universe exactly as it should be. I was grateful for the opportunity to do that."

He returned to the entrance hall, expecting the armed guard to be awakening from his torpor. But Dudley Prince was still a statue, still convinced that, if he budged, he would find himself back in prison again.

Trout again confronted him, saying, "Wake up! Wake up! You've got free will again, and there's work to do!" And so on.

Nothing.

Trout had an inspiration! Instead of trying to sell the concept of free will, which he himself didn't believe in, he said this: "You've been very sick! Now you're well again. You've been very sick! Now you're well again."

That mantra worked!

Trout could have been a great advertising man. The same has been said of Jesus Christ. The basis of every great advertisement is a *credible promise*. Jesus promised better times in an afterlife. Trout was promising the same thing in the here and now.

Dudley Prince's spiritual rigor mortis began to thaw! Trout hastened his recovery by telling him to snap his fingers and stamp his feet, and stick out his tongue and wiggle his butt, and so on.

Trout, who had never even earned a High School Equivalency Certificate, had nonetheless become a real-life Dr. Frankenstein!

47

Uncle Alex Vonnegut, who said we should exclaim out loud whenever we were accidentally happy, was considered a fool by his wife, Aunt Raye. He certainly started out as a fool when a spanking-new freshman at Harvard. Uncle Alex was asked to explain in an essay why he had come to Harvard all the way from Indianapolis. By his own gleeful account, he wrote, "Because my big brother is at MIT."

He never had a kid, and never owned a gun. He owned a lot of books, though, and kept buying new ones, and giving me those he thought were particularly well done. It was an ordeal for him to find this book or that one, so he could read some particularly magical passage aloud to me. Here's why: His wife Aunt Raye, who was said to be artistic, arranged his library according to the size and color of the volumes, and stairstep style.

So he might say of a collection of essays by his hero H. L. Mencken, "I think it was green, and about *this* high."

· · · · ·

His sister, my aunt Irma, said to me one time when I was a grownup, "*All* Vonnegut men are scared to death of women." Her two brothers were sure as heck scared of *her.*

Listen: A Harvard education for my Uncle Alex wasn't the trophy of a micromanaged Darwinian victory over others that it is today. His father, the architect Bernard Vonnegut, sent him there in order that he might become *civilized,* which he did indeed become, although fabulously henpecked, and nothing more than a life insurance salesman.

I am eternally grateful to him, and indirectly to what Harvard used to be, I suppose, for my knack of finding in great books, some of them very funny books, reason enough to feel honored to be alive, no matter what else may be going on.

It now appears that books in the form so beloved by Uncle Alex and me, hinged and unlocked boxes, packed with leaves speckled by ink, are obsolescent. My grandchildren are already doing much of their reading from words projected on the face of a video screen.

Please, please, please wait just a minute!

At the time of their invention, books were devices as crassly practical for storing or transmitting language, albeit fabricated from scarcely modified substances found in forest and field and animals, as the latest Silicon Valley miracles. But by accident, not by cunning calculation, books, because of their weight and texture, and because of their sweetly token resistance to manipulation, involve our hands and eyes, and then our minds and souls, in a spiritual adventure I would be very sorry for my grandchildren not to know about.

48

It is piquant to me that one of the greatest poets and one of the greatest playwrights of this century would both deny that they were from the Middle West, specifically from St. Louis, Missouri. I mean T. S. Eliot, who wound up sounding like the Archbishop of Canterbury, and Tennessee Williams, a product of Washington University in St. Louis and the University of Iowa, who wound up sounding like Ashley Wilkes in *Gone With the Wind*.

True enough, Williams was born in Mississippi, but moved to St. Louis when he was seven. And it was he who named himself Tennessee when he was twenty-seven. Before he did that to himself, he was Tom.

Cole Porter was born in Peru, Indiana, pronounced PEE-roo. "Night and Day"? "Begin the Beguine"? Not bad, not bad.

Kilgore Trout was born in a hospital in Bermuda, near where his father, Raymond, was gathering material for a follow-up on his doctoral dissertation on the last of the Bermuda Erns. The sole remaining rookery of those great blue birds, the largest of all pelagic raptors, was on Dead Man's Rock, an otherwise uninhabited lava steeple in the center of the notorious Bermuda Triangle. Trout was in fact conceived on Dead Man's Rock during his parents' honeymoon.

What was particularly interesting about these erns was that the female birds, and not anything people had done, so far as anybody could tell, were to blame for the rapidly dwindling population. In the past, and presumably for thousands of years, the females had hatched their eggs, and tended the young, and finally taught them to fly by kicking them off the top of the steeple.

But when Raymond Trout went there as a doctoral candidate with his bride, he found that the females had taken to bowdlerizing the nurturing process by kicking the eggs off the top of the steeple.

Thus did Kilgore Trout's father providentially become a specialist, thanks to the female Bermuda Erns' initiative, or whatever you want to call it, in evolutionary mechanisms governing fates of species, mechanisms other than the Occam's Razor of Darwin's *Natural Selection*.

Nothing would do, then, but that the Trout family, when little Kilgore was nine, spend the summer of 1926 camped on the shore of Disappointment Lake in inland Nova Scotia. The Dalhousie Woodpeckers in that area had quit the brain-rattling business of pecking wood, and were feasting on the plentiful blackflies on the backs of deer and moose instead.

Dalhousies, of course, are the commonest woodpeckers in eastern Canada, mainly, ranging from Newfoundland to Manitoba, and from Hudson Bay to Detroit, Michigan. Only those around Disappointment Lake, however, identical with the rest in plumage and beak size and shape, and so on, had stopped getting at bugs the hard way, digging them out one at a time, from holes the bugs had made or found in tree trunks.

They were first observed gorging on blackflies in 1916, with World War One going on in the other hemisphere. The Disappointment Lake Dalhousies, however, were not subjected to observation year after year before that, or since. This was because the clouds of voracious blackflies, often resembling little tornadoes, according to Trout, made the apostate Dalhousies' habitat virtually uninhabitable by human beings.

So the Trout family spent the summer up there dressed like beekeepers night and day, in gloves, in long-sleeved shirts tied at the wrists, and long pants tied at the ankles, in wide-brimmed hats draped with gauze, to protect their heads and necks, no matter how hellishly hot the weather. Father, mother, and son dragged the camping gear and a heavy motion picture camera and tripod to the marshy campsite while harnessed to a travois.

Dr. Trout expected to film nothing more than ordinary Dalhousies, indistinguishable from other Dalhousies, but pecking at the backs of deer and moose instead of tree trunks. Such simple pictures would have been exciting enough, showing that lower animals were capable of cultural as well as biological evolution. One might have extrapolated from them the supposition that one bird in the flock was a sort of Albert Einstein, so to speak, having theorized and then proved that blackflies were as nutritious as anything that could be dug out of a tree trunk.

Was Dr. Trout ever in for a surprise, though! Not only were these birds obscenely fat, and thus easy prey for predators. They were exploding, too! Spores from a tree fungus growing near Dalhousie nests found an opportunity to become a new disease in the intestinal tracts of the overweight birds, thanks to certain chemicals in the bodies of black-flies.

The new life-style of the fungus inside the birds at one point triggered the sudden release of quantities of carbon dioxide so copious that the birds blew up! One Dalhousie, perhaps the last veteran of the Disappointment Lake experiment, would explode a year later in a park in Detroit, Michigan, setting off the second-worst race riot in the Motor City's history.

49

Trout wrote a story one time about another race riot. It was on a planet twice as big as Earth, orbiting Puke, a star the size of a BB, two billion years ago.

I asked my big brother Bernie in the American Museum of Natural History in New York, and this was long before the period of the rerun, whether he believed in Darwin's theory of evolution. He said he did, and I asked how come, and he said, "Because it's the only game in town."

Bernie's reply is the tag line of yet another joke from long ago, like "Ting-a-ling, you son of a bitch!" It seems a guy is off to play cards, and a friend tells him the game is crooked. The guy says, "Yeah, I know, but it's the only game in town."

I am too lazy to chase down the exact quotation, but the British astronomer Fred Hoyle said something to this effect: That believing in

162

Darwin's theoretical mechanisms of evolution was like believing that a hurricane could blow through a junkyard and build a Boeing 747.

No matter what is doing the creating, I have to say that the giraffe and the rhinoceros are ridiculous.

And so is the human brain, capable, in cahoots with the more sensitive parts of the body, such as the ding-dong, of hating life while pretending to love it, and behaving accordingly: "Somebody shoot me while I'm happy!"

Kilgore Trout, the ornithologist's son, wrote in *My Ten Years on Automatic Pilot*: "The *Fiduciary* is a mythological bird. It has never existed in Nature, never could, never will."

Trout is the only person who ever said a fiduciary was any sort of bird. The noun (from the Latin *fiducia*, confidence, trust) in fact identifies a sort of *Homo sapiens* who will conserve the property, and nowadays especially paper or computer representations of wealth, belonging to other people, including the treasuries of their governments.

He or she or it cannot exist, thanks to the brain and the ding-dong, et cetera. So we have in this summer of 1996, rerun or not, and as always, faithless custodians of capital making themselves multimillionaires and multibillionaires, while playing beanbag with money better spent on creating meaningful jobs and training people to fill them, and raising our young and retiring our old in surroundings of respect and safety.

For Christ's sake, let's help more of our frightened people get through this thing, whatever it is.

Why throw money at problems? That is what money is *for*.

Should the nation's wealth be redistributed? It has been and continues to be redistributed to a few people in a manner strikingly un-helpful.

Let me note that Kilgore Trout and I have never used semicolons. They don't do anything, don't suggest anything. They are transvestite hermaphrodites.

Yes, and any dream of taking better care of our people might as well be a transvestite hermaphrodite without some scheme for giving us all the support and companionship of extended families, within which sharing and compassion are more plausible than in an enormous nation, and a *Fiduciary* may not be as mythical as the *Roc* and the *Phoenix* after all.

50

I am so old that I can remember when the word *fuck* was thought to be so full of bad magic that no respectable publication would print it. Another old joke: "Don't say 'fuck' in front of the B-A-B-Y."

A word just as full of poison, supposedly, but which could be spoken in polite company, provided the speaker's tone implied fear and loathing, was *Communism*, denoting an activity as commonly and innocently practiced in many primitive societies as fucking.

So it was a particularly elegant commentary on the patriotism and nice-nellyism during the deliberately insane Vietnam War when the satirist Paul Krassner printed red-white-and-blue bumper stickers that said FUCK COMMUNISM!

My novel *Slaughterhouse-Five* was attacked back then for containing the word *motherfucker*. In an early episode, somebody takes a shot at four American soldiers caught behind the German lines. One American snarls at another one, who, as I say, has never fucked anyone, "Get your head down, you dumb motherfucker."

Ever since those words were published, mothers of sons have had to wear chastity belts while doing housework.

I of course understand that the widespread revulsion inspired even now, and perhaps forever, by the word *Communism* is a sane response to the cruelties and stupidities of the dictators of the USSR, who called themselves, hey presto, *Communists,* just as Hitler called himself, hey presto, a *Christian.*

To children of the Great Depression, however, it still seems a mild shame to outlaw from polite thought, because of the crimes of tyrants, a word that in the beginning described for us nothing more than a possibly reasonable alternative to the Wall Street crapshoot.

Yes, and the word *Socialist* was the second *S* in *USSR,* so good-bye, *Socialism* along with *Communism,* good-bye to the soul of Eugene Debs of Terre Haute, Indiana, where the moonlight's shining bright along the Wabash. From the fields there comes the breath of new-mown hay.

"While there is a soul in prison, I am not free."

The Great Depression was a time for discussing all sorts of alternatives to the Wall Street crapshoot, which had suddenly killed so many businesses, including banks. The crapshoot left millions and millions of Americans without any way to pay for food and shelter and clothing.

So what?

That was almost a century ago, if you want to count the rerun. Forget it! Practically everybody who was alive back then is deader than a mackerel. Happy Socialism to them in the Afterlife!

What matters now is that, on the afternoon of February 13th, 2001,

Kilgore Trout roused Dudley Prince from his Post-Timequake Apathy. Trout urged him to speak, to say anything, no matter how nonsensical. Trout suggested he say, "I pledge allegiance to the flag," or whatever, to prove to himself thereby that he was again in charge of his own destiny.

Prince spoke groggily at first. He didn't pledge allegiance, but indicated instead that he was trying to understand everything Trout had said to him so far. He said, "You told me I *had* something."

"You were sick, but now you're well, and there's work to do," said Trout.

"Before that," said Prince. "You said I *had* something."

"Forget it," said Trout. "I was all excited. I wasn't making sense."

"I still want to know what you said I *had*," said Prince.

"I said you had free will," said Trout.

"Free will, free will, free will," echoed Prince with wry wonderment. "I always wondered what it was I *had*. Now I got a *name* for it."

"Please forget what I said," said Trout. "There are lives to save!"

"You know what you can do with free will?" said Prince.

"No," said Trout.

"You can stuff it up your ass," said Prince.

51

When I liken Trout there in the entrance hall of the American Academy of Arts and Letters, awakening Dudley Prince from PTA, to Dr. Frankenstein, I am alluding of course to the antihero of the novel *Frankenstein—or, The Modern Prometheus,* by Mary Wollstonecraft Shelley, second wife of the English poet Percy Bysshe Shelley. In that book, the scientist Frankenstein puts a bunch of body parts from different corpses together in the shape of a man.

Frankenstein jazzes them with electricity. The results in the book are exact opposites of those since achieved in real-life American state penitentiaries with real-life electric chairs. Most people think Frankenstein is the monster. He isn't. Frankenstein is the scientist.

Prometheus in Greek mythology makes the first human beings from mud. He steals fire from Heaven and gives it to them so they can be warm and cook, and not, one would hope, so we could incinerate all the little yellow bastards in Hiroshima and Nagasaki, which are in Japan.

In chapter 2 of this wonderful book of mine, I mention a commemoration in the chapel of the University of Chicago of the fiftieth anniversary of the atom-bombing of Hiroshima. I said at the time that I had to respect the opinion of my friend William Styron that the Hiroshima bomb saved his life. Styron was then a United States Marine, training for an invasion of the Japanese home islands, when that bomb was dropped.

I had to add, though, that I knew a single word that proved our democratic government was capable of committing obscene, gleefully rabid and racist, yahooistic murders of unarmed men, women, and children, murders wholly devoid of military common sense. I said the word. It was a foreign word. That word was *Nagasaki.*

Whatever! That, too, was a long, long time ago, and ten years longer ago than that, if you want to count the rerun. What I find worth exclaiming about right now is the continuing applicability to the human condition, years after free will has ceased to be a novelty, of what jazzed Dudley Prince back to life, of what is now known generally as Kilgore's Creed: "You were sick, but now you're well again, and there's work to do."

Teachers in public schools across the land, I hear, say Kilgore's Creed to students after the students have recited the Pledge of Allegiance and the Lord's Prayer at the beginning of each school day. Teachers say it seems to help.

A friend told me he was at a wedding where the minister said at the climax of the ceremony: "You were sick, but now you're well again, and there's work to do. I now pronounce you man and wife."

Another friend, a biochemist for a cat food company, said she was staying at a hotel in Toronto, Canada, and she asked the front desk to give her a wake-up call in the morning. She answered her phone the next morning, and the operator said, "You were sick, but now you're well again, and there's work to do. It's seven a.m., and the temperature outside is thirty-two degrees Fahrenheit, or zero Celsius."

On the afternoon of February 13th, 2001, alone, and then during the next two weeks or so, Kilgore's Creed did as much to save life on Earth as Einstein's *E equals mc squared* had done to end it two generations earlier.

Trout had Dudley Prince say the magic words to the other two armed guards on the day shift at the Academy. They went into the former Museum of the American Indian, and said them to the catatonic bums in there. A goodly number of the aroused sacred cattle, maybe a third of them, became anti-PTA evangelists in turn. Armed with nothing more than Kilgore's Creed, these ragged veterans of unemployability fanned out through the neighborhood to convert more living statues to lives of usefulness, to helping the injured, or at least getting them the hell indoors somewhere before they froze to death.

"God is in the details," Anonymous tells us in the sixteenth edition of *Bartlett's Familiar Quotations*. The seemingly pipsqueak detail of what became of the armored limousine that delivered Zoltan Pepper to be creamed by the hook-and-ladder as he rang the doorbell of the Academy is a case in point. The limousine driver, Jerry Rivers, had moved it fifty yards to the west, toward the Hudson River, after unloading his paraplegic passenger and his wheelchair on the sidewalk.

That was still part of the rerun. Rerun or not, though, Jerry wasn't to stay parked in front of the Academy, lest the luxury vehicle arouse suspicions that the Academy might not be an abandoned building after all. If that hadn't been the policy, the limousine would have absorbed the impact of the fire truck, and possibly but not certainly saved the life of Zoltan Pepper as he rang the doorbell.

But at what cost? The entrance to the Academy would not have been broached, giving Kilgore Trout access to Dudley Prince and the other armed guards. Trout could not have put on a spare guard's uniform he found in there, which made him look like an authority figure. He would not have been able to arm himself with the Academy's bazooka, with which he knocked out the braying burglar alarms of impacted but unoccupied parked vehicles.

52

The American Academy of Arts and Letters owned a bazooka because the warlords who knocked over Columbia University spearheaded their attack with a tank stolen from the Rainbow Division of the National Guard. They were so audacious that they flew *Old Glory, The Stars and Stripes*.

It is conceivable that the warlords, with whom nobody messes, any more than anybody messes with the ten biggest corporations, consider themselves as American as anyone. "America," wrote Kilgore Trout in *MTYOAP*, "is the interplay of three hundred million Rube Goldberg contraptions invented only yesterday.

"And you better have an extended family," he added, although he himself had done without one between the time he was discharged from the Army, on September 11th, 1945, and March 1st, 2001, the day he and Monica Pepper and Dudley Prince and Jerry Rivers arrived by armored limousine, with an overloaded trailer wallowing behind, at Xanadu.

. . . . .

Rube Goldberg was a newspaper cartoonist during the terminal century of the previous Christian millennium. He drew pictures of absurdly complex and undependable machines, employing treadmills and trapdoors and bells and whistles, and domestic animals in harness and blowtorches and mailmen and light bulbs, and firecrackers and mirrors and radios and Victrolas, and pistols firing blank cartridges, and so on, in order to accomplish some simple task, such as closing a window blind.

Yes, and Trout harped on the human need for extended families, and I still do, because it is so obvious that we, because we are human, need them as much as we need proteins and carbohydrates and fats and vitamins and essential minerals.

I have just read about a teenage father who shook his baby to death because it couldn't control its anal sphincter yet and wouldn't stop crying. In an extended family, there would have been other people around, who would have rescued and comforted the baby, and the father, too.

If the father had been raised in an extended family, he might not have been such an awful father, or maybe not a father at all yet, because he was still too young to be a good one, or because he was too crazy to *ever* be a good one.

I was in southern Nigeria in 1970, at the very end of the Biafran War there, on the Biafran side, the losing side, the mostly Ibo side, long before the rerun. I met an Ibo father of a new baby. He had four hundred relatives! Even with a losing war going on, he and his wife were about to go on a trip, introducing the baby to all its relatives.

When the Biafran army needed replacements, big Ibo families met to decide who should go. In peacetime, the families met to decide who should go to college, often to Cal Tech or Oxford or Harvard, a long way off. And then a whole family chipped in to pay for the travel and tuition and clothing suitable for the climate and dominant society where a kid was going next.

I met the Ibo writer Chinua Achebe over there. He is teaching and writing at Bard College in Annandale-on-Hudson, New York, 12504, over here now. I asked him how the Ibos were now, with Nigeria run by a rapacious junta which regularly hangs its critics for having much too much free will.

Chinua said no Ibos had roles in the government, nor did they want any. He said Ibos survived in modest businesses unlikely to bring them into conflict with the government or its friends, which included representatives of Shell Oil Company.

They must have held many meetings, in which ethics as well as survival schemes were debated.

And they still send their smartest kids off to the best universities far away.

When I celebrate the idea of a family and family values, I don't mean a man and a woman and their kids, new in town, scared to death, and not knowing whether to shit or go blind in the midst of economic and technological and ecological and political chaos. I'm talking about what so many Americans need so frantically: what I had in Indianapolis before World War Two, and what the characters in Thornton Wilder's *Our Town* had, and what the Ibos have.

. . . . .

In chapter 45, I proposed two amendments to the Constitution. Here are two more, little enough to expect from life, one would think, like the Bill of Rights:

Article XXX: Every person, upon reaching a statutory age of puberty, shall be declared an adult in a solemn public ritual, during which he or she must welcome his or her new responsibilities in the community, and their attendant dignities.

Article XXXI: Every effort shall be made to make every person feel that he or she will be sorely missed when he or she is gone.

Such essential elements in an ideal diet for a human spirit, of course, can be provided convincingly only by extended families.

53

The monster in *Frankenstein—or, The Modern Prometheus* turns mean because he finds it so humiliating to be alive and yet so ugly, so *unpopular*. He kills Frankenstein, who, again, is the scientist and not the monster. And let me hasten to say that my big brother Bernie never has been a Frankenstein-style scientist, never has worked nor would have worked on purposely destructive devices of any sort. He hasn't been a Pandora, either, turning loose new poisons or new diseases or whatever.

According to Greek mythology, Pandora was the first woman. She was made by the gods who were angry with Prometheus for making a man out of mud and then stealing fire from them. Making a woman was their *revenge*. They gave Pandora a box. Prometheus begged her not to open it. She opened it. Every evil to which human flesh is heir came out of it.

The last thing to come out of the box was *hope*. It flew away.

I didn't make that depressing story up. Neither did Kilgore Trout. Ancient Greeks did.

. . . . .

This is the point I want to make, though: Frankenstein's monster was unhappy and destructive, whereas the people Trout energized in the neighborhood of the Academy, although most of them wouldn't have won any beauty contests, were by and large cheerful and public-spirited.

I have to say *most of them* wouldn't have won any beauty contests. There was at least one strikingly beautiful woman involved. That was a member of the Academy's office staff. That was Clara Zine. Monica Pepper is certain that Clara Zine was the one who was smoking the cigar that set off the smoke alarm in the picture gallery. When confronted by Monica, Clara Zine swore that in her whole life she had never smoked a cigar, that she hated cigars, and she disappeared.

I have no idea what has become of her.

Clara Zine and Monica were tending the wounded in the former Museum of the American Indian, which Trout had turned into a hospital, when Monica asked Clara about the cigar, and then Clara departed in a huffmobile.

Trout, carrying what had become *his* bazooka, and accompanied by Dudley Prince and the other two armed guards, had thrown out all the bums who were still in the shelter. They did that in order to free up the cots for people with broken limbs or skulls or whatever, who needed and deserved to lie down where it was warm even more than the bums did.

It was triage, such as Kilgore Trout had seen practiced on World War Two battlefields. "I only regret that I have but one life to lose for my country," said the American patriot Nathan Hale. "Fuck the bums!" said the American patriot Kilgore Trout.

. . . . .

It was Jerry Rivers, the chauffeur of the Peppers' stretch limousine, however, who steered his dreamboat around wrecked vehicles and their victims, often driving on sidewalks, to reach the studios of the Columbia Broadcasting System down on West 52nd Street. Rivers awakened the staff there with, "You were sick, but now you're well again, and there's work to do." And then he got them to broadcast that same message on both radio and TV from coast to coast.

In order to get them to do that, though, he had to tell them a lie. He said everybody was recovering from a nerve gas attack by persons unknown. So the first version of Kilgore's Creed to reach millions in the nation, and then billions in the world, was this: "This is a CBS exclusive! There has been a nerve gas attack by persons unknown. You were sick, but now you're well again, and there's work to do. Make sure all children and senior citizens are safe indoors."

54

Certainly! Mistakes were made! But Trout's silencing of automobile burglar alarms with his bazooka wasn't one of them. If a manual is to be written about how to behave in urban areas should there be another timequake, and then a rerun, and then free will kicks in again, it should recommend that every neighborhood have a bazooka, and that responsible adults know where it is.

Mistakes? The manual should point out that vehicles themselves *are not responsible* for the damage they cause, whether controlled or not. Punishing automobiles as though they were rebellious slaves in need of a hiding is a waste of time! Scapegoating cars and trucks and buses still in running condition, simply because they are *automobiles*, moreover, deprives rescue workers and refugees of their means of transportation.

As Trout advises in *MTYOAP*: "Beating the daylights out of a stranger's parked Dodge Intrepid may well afford fleeting relief from symptoms of stress. When all is said and done, though, that can only leave the life of its owner even more of a crock of shit than it was before. Do unto others' vehicles as you would have them do unto yours.

"It is pure superstition that a motor vehicle with its ignition turned

179

off can start itself up without the help of a human being," he goes on. "If, after free will kicks in, you *must* yank the ignition keys out of driverless vehicles whose engines aren't running, please, please, please throw the keys into a *mailbox,* and not down a storm sewer or into a trash-strewn vacant lot."

The biggest mistake Trout himself made, probably, was in turning the American Academy of Arts and Letters into a morgue. The steel front door and its frame were tacked up back in place again, to keep the heat inside. It would have made more sense to line up the bodies outside, where the temperature was well below freezing.

And Trout couldn't have been expected to worry about it, way-the-hell-and-gone up there on West 155th, but some awakened member of the Federal Aviation Administration should have realized, after all the crashing at ground level petered out, that there were still planes aloft on automatic pilot. Their crews and passengers, still gaga with untreated PTA, couldn't care doodley what would happen when the fuel ran out.

In ten minutes, or maybe an hour, or maybe three hours or whatever, their heavier-than-air-craft, often six miles up, would *cash in the chips,* would *buy the farm,* for all aboard.

For the Mbuti, the rain forest Pygmies of Zaire, Africa, February 13th, 2001, was in all probability a day neither more nor less amazing than any other day, unless a rogue airplane happened to land on top of one of them after the rerun stopped.

The worst of all aircraft when free will kicks in, of course, are helicopters, or *choppers,* air screws first envisioned by the genius Leonardo da Vinci (1452–1519). Choppers can't glide. Choppers don't want to fly in the first place.

A safer place than a helicopter aloft is a roller coaster or a Ferris wheel.

Yes, and when martial law was established in New York City, the former Museum of the American Indian was turned into a barracks, and Kilgore Trout was relieved of his bazooka, and the Academy's headquarters were requisitioned as an officers' club, and he and Monica Pepper and Dudley Prince and Jerry Rivers took off in the limousine for Xanadu.

Trout, the former hobo, had expensive clothing, including shoes and socks and underwear and cuff links, and matched Louis Vuitton luggage which had belonged to Zoltan Pepper. Everybody agreed that Monica's husband was better off dead. What would he have had to look forward to?

When Trout found Zoltan's flattened and elongated wheelchair in the middle of West 155th Street, he leaned it against a tree and said it was modern art. The two wheels had been squashed together so they looked like one. Trout said it was a six-foot aluminum-and-leather praying mantis, trying to ride a unicycle.

He called it *The Spirit of the Twenty-first Century.*

55

I met the author Dick Francis at the Kentucky Derby years ago. I knew he had been a champion rider in steeplechases. I said he was a bigger man than I had expected. He replied that it took a big man to "hold a horse together" in a steeplechase. This image of his remained in the forefront of my memory so long, I think, because life itself can seem a lot like that: a matter of holding one's self-respect together, instead of a horse, as one's self-respect is expected to hurdle fences and hedges and water.

My dear thirteen-year-old daughter Lily, having become a pretty adolescent, appears to me, as do most American adolescents, to be holding her self-respect together the best she can in a really scary steeplechase.

I said to the new graduates at Butler University, not much older than Lily, that they were being called *Generation X*, two clicks from the end, but that they were as much *Generation A* as Adam and Eve had been. What malarkey!

Esprit de l'escalier! Better late than never! Only at this very moment in 1996, as I am about to write the next sentence, have I realized how meaningless the image of a Garden of Eden must have been to my young audience, since the world was so densely populated with other secretly frightened people, and so overplanted and rigged with both natural and manmade booby traps.

The next sentence: I should have told them they were like Dick Francis when Dick Francis was young, and astride an animal full of pride and panic, in the starting gate for a steeplechase.

More: If a steed balks again and again at hazards, it is put out to pasture. The self-respects of most middle-class American people my age or older, and still alive, are out to pasture now, not a bad place to be. They munch. They ruminate.

If self-respect breaks a leg, the leg can never heal. Its owner has to shoot it. My mother and Ernest Hemingway and my former literary agent and Jerzy Kosinski and my reluctant thesis advisor at the University of Chicago and Eva Braun all come to mind.

But not Kilgore Trout. His indestructible self-respect is what I loved most about Kilgore Trout. Men loving men can happen, in peacetime as well as war. I also loved my war buddy Bernard V. O'Hare.

Many people fail because their brains, their three-and-a-half-pound blood-soaked sponges, their dogs' breakfasts, don't work well enough. The cause of a failure can be as simple as that. Some people, try as they may, can't cut the mustard! That's that!

I have a male cousin my age who was doing miserably back in Shortridge High School He was a hulking interior lineman, and very sweet. He brought home an awful report card. His father asked him, "What is the *meaning* of this?" My cousin responded as follows: "Don't you *know*, Father? I'm dumb, I'm *dumb*."

Put this in your pipe and smoke it: My maternal great-uncle Carl Barus was a founder and president of the American Physical Society. A building at Brown University is named in his honor. Uncle Carl Barus was a professor there for many years. I never met him. My big brother did. Until this summer of 1996, Bernie and I had thought of him as a serene contributor to modest but tidy increases in human understanding of the laws of Nature.

Last June, though, I asked Bernie to tell me some specific discoveries, however small, made by our distinguished great-uncle, whose genes Bernie had inherited so outstandingly. Bernie's response was anything but *schnip-schnop*, anything but prompt. Bernie was bemused to realize at such a late date that Uncle Carl, while making a career in physics attractive, had never told him about anything he himself had accomplished.

"I'll have to look him up," said Bernie.

Hold on to your hats!

Listen: Uncle Carl, in 1900 or thereabouts, experimented with the effects of X rays and radioactivity on condensation in a cloud chamber, a wooden cylinder filled with a fog he himself had concocted. He concluded and published as a certainty that ionization was relatively unimportant in condensation.

At about the same time, friends and neighbors, the Scottish physicist Charles Thomson Rees Wilson performed similar experiments with a cloud chamber made of *glass*. The canny Scot proved that ions produced by X rays and radioactivity had a lot to do with condensation. He criticized Uncle Carl for ignoring contamination from the wood walls of his chamber, for his crude method of making clouds, and for not shielding his fog from the electrical field of his X-ray apparatus.

Wilson went on to make paths of electrically charged particles visible to the naked eye by means of his cloud chamber. In 1927, he shared a Nobel Prize for Physics for doing this.

Uncle Carl must have felt like something the cat drug in!

56

A Luddite to the end, as was Kilgore Trout, as was Ned Ludd, the possibly but not certainly fictitious workman who smashed up machinery, supposedly, in Leicestershire, England, at the beginning of the nineteenth century, I persist in pecking away at a manual typewriter. That still leaves me technologically several generations ahead of William Styron and Stephen King, who, like Trout, write with pens on yellow legal pads.

I correct my pages with pen or pencil. I have come into Manhattan on business. I telephone a woman who has been doing my retyping for years and years now. She doesn't have a computer, either. Maybe I should can her. She has moved from the city to a country town. I ask her what the weather is like out that way. I ask if there have been any unusual birds at her bird feeder. I ask if squirrels have found a way to get at it, and so on.

Yes, the squirrels have found a new way to get at the feeder. They can become trapeze artists, if they have to.

She has had back trouble in the past. I ask her how her back is. She says her back is OK. She asks how my daughter Lily is. I say Lily is OK. She asks how old Lily is now, and I say she'll be fourteen in December.

She says, "Fourteen! My gosh, my gosh. It seems like only yesterday she was just a little baby."

I say I have a few more pages for her to type. She says, "Good." I will have to mail them to her, since she doesn't have a fax. Again: Maybe I should can her.

I am still on the third floor of our brownstone in the city, and we don't have an elevator. So down the stairs I go with my pages, *clumpity, clumpity, clumpity.* I get down to the first floor, where my wife has her office. Her favorite reading when she was Lily's age was stories about Nancy Drew, the girl detective.

Nancy Drew is to Jill what Kilgore Trout is to me, so Jill says, "Where are you going?"

I say, "I am going to buy an envelope."

She says, "You are not a poor man. Why don't you buy a thousand envelopes and put them in a closet?" She thinks she is being logical. She has a computer. She has a fax. She has an answering machine on her telephone, so she doesn't miss any important messages. She has a Xerox. She has all that garbage.

I say, "I'll be back real soon."

Out into the world I go! Muggers! Autograph hounds! Junkies! People with real jobs! Maybe an easy lay! United Nations functionaries and diplomats!

Our house is near the UN, so there are all kinds of really foreign-looking people getting in or out of illegally parked limousines, doing the best they can, like all the rest of us, to hold their self-respect together. As I saunter a half-block to the news store on Second Avenue, which also sells stationery, I can feel, if I so choose, because of all the foreigners, like Humphrey Bogart or Peter Lorre in *Casablanca,* the third-greatest movie ever made.

The greatest movie ever, as anybody with half a brain knows, is *My Life as a Dog.* The second-greatest movie ever is *All About Eve.*

There is a chance, moreover, that I will see Katharine Hepburn, a *real* movie star! She lives only one block from us! When I speak to her, and tell her my name, she always says, "Oh yes, you're that friend of my brother's." I do not know her brother.

No such luck today, though, but what the heck. I am a philosopher. I have to be.

Into the news store I go. Relatively poor people, with lives not strikingly worth living, are lined up to buy lottery tickets or other crap. All keep their cool. They pretend they don't know I'm a celebrity.

The store is a Ma-and-Pa joint owned by *Hindus,* honest-to-God *Hindus!* The woman has a teeny-weeny ruby between her eyes. That's worth a trip. Who needs an envelope?

You must remember this, a kiss is still a kiss, a sigh is still a sigh.

I know the Hindus' stock of stationery as well as they do. I didn't study anthropology for nothing. I find one nine-by-twelve manila envelope without assistance, remembering simultaneously a joke about the Chicago Cubs baseball team. The Cubs were supposedly moving to the Philippine Islands, where they would be renamed the Manila Folders. That would have been a good joke about the Boston Red Sox, too.

I take my place at the end of the line, chatting with fellow customers who are buying something other than lottery tickets. The lottery ticket suckers, decorticated by hope and numerology, may as well be victims of Post-Timequake Apathy. You could run them over with an eighteen-wheeler. They wouldn't care.

57

From the news store I go one block south to the Postal Convenience Station, where I am secretly in love with a woman behind the counter. I have already put my pages in the manila envelope. I address it, and then I take my place at the end of another long line. What I need now is postage! Yum, yum, yum!

The woman I love there does not know I love her. You want to talk about poker faces? When her eyes meet mine, she might as well be looking at a cantaloupe!

Because she works sitting down, and because of the counter and the smock she wears, all I have ever seen of her is from the neck up. That's enough! From the neck up she is like a Thanksgiving dinner! I don't mean she looks like a plateful of turkey and sweet potatoes and cranberry sauce. I mean she makes me feel like that is what has just been set before me. Dig in! Dig in!

Unadorned, I believe, her neck and face and ears and hair would still be Thanksgiving dinner. Every day, though, she hangs new dingle-dangles from her ears and around her neck. Sometimes her hair is up, sometimes it's down. Sometimes it's frizzy, sometimes it's straight.

What she can't do with just her eyes and lips! One day I'm buying a stamp from Count Dracula's daughter! The next day she's the Virgin Mary.

This time she's Ingrid Bergman in *Stromboli*. But she is a long way off still. There are many addled old poops, no good at counting money anymore, and immigrants talking gibberish, maddeningly imagining it to be English, in line ahead of me.

One time I had my pocket picked in that Postal Convenience Center. Convenient for whom?

I put the waiting time to good use. I learn about stupid bosses and jobs I will never have, and about parts of the world I will never see, and about diseases I hope I will never have, and about different kinds of dogs people have owned, and so on. By means of a computer? No. I do it by means of the lost art of conversation.

I at last have my envelope weighed and stamped by the only woman in the whole wide world who could make me sincerely happy. With her I wouldn't have to *fake* it.

I go home. I have had one heck of a good time. Listen: We are here on Earth to fart around. Don't let anybody tell you any different!

58

I have taught creative writing during my seventy-three years on automatic pilot, rerun or not. I did it first at the University of Iowa in 1965. After that came Harvard, and then the City College of New York. I don't do it anymore.

I taught how to be sociable with ink on paper. I told my students that when they were writing they should be good dates on blind dates, should show strangers good times. Alternatively, they should run really nice whorehouses, come one, come all, although they were in fact working in perfect solitude. I said I expected them to do this with nothing but idiosyncratic arrangements in horizontal lines of twenty-six phonetic symbols, ten numbers, and maybe eight punctuation marks, because it wasn't anything that hadn't been done before.

In 1996, with movies and TV doing such good jobs of holding the attention of literates and illiterates alike, I have to question the value of my very strange, when you think about it, charm school. There *is* this: Attempted seductions with nothing but words on paper are so *cheap* for would-be ink-stained Don Juans or Cleopatras! They don't have to get a bankable actor or actress to commit to the project, and then a bankable director, and so on, and then raise millions and millions of buckareenies from manic-depressive experts on what most people want.

Still and all, why bother? Here's *my* answer: Many people need desperately to receive this message: "I feel and think much as you do, care about many of the things you care about, although most people don't care about them. You are not alone."

Steve Adams, one of my three adopted nephews, was a successful TV comedy writer in Los Angeles, California, a few years back. His big brother Jim is an ex–Peace Corps guy and now a psychiatric nurse. His kid brother Kurt is a veteran pilot with Continental Airlines, with scrambled eggs on his cap, gold braid on his sleeves. All Steve's kid brother ever wanted to do for a living was fly. A dream came true!

Steve learned the hard way that all his jokes for TV had to be about events that had been made much of by TV itself, and very *recently*. If a joke was about something that hadn't been on TV for a month or more, the watchers wouldn't have a clue, even though the laugh track was laughing, as to what they themselves were supposed to laugh about.

Guess what? TV is an *eraser*.

Having even the immediate past erased may indeed make it more comfortable for most people to get through this thing, whatever it is. Jane, my first wife, won her Phi Beta Kappa key at Swarthmore College over the objections of the History Department. She had written, and then argued in oral examinations, that all that could be learned from history was that history itself was absolutely nonsensical, so study something else, like music.

I agreed with her, and so would have Kilgore Trout. But history still hadn't been erased back then. And when I started out as a writer, I could refer to events and personalities in the past, even the distant past, with a reasonable expectation that a fair number of readers would respond with some emotion, whether positive or negative, when I mentioned them.

Case in point: The murder of the greatest President this country will ever have, Abraham Lincoln, by the twenty-six-year-old ham actor John Wilkes Booth.

That assassination was a major event in *Timequake One*. Who is there left under the age of sixty, and not in a History Department, to give a damn?

59

Elias Pembroke, a fictitious Rhode Island naval architect who was Abraham Lincoln's Assistant Secretary of the Navy during our Civil War, was a character in *Timequake One*. I said he made significant contributions to the design of the power train of the ironclad warship *Monitor*, but was neglectful of his wife, Julia, who fell in love with a dashing young actor and rakehell named John Wilkes Booth.

Julia wrote love letters to Booth. A tryst was arranged for April 14th, 1863, two years before Booth shot Lincoln from behind with a derringer. She went to New York City from Washington with a chaperone, the alcoholic wife of an admiral, ostensibly to shop, and to escape the tensions in the besieged capital. They checked into the hotel where Booth was staying, and attended his performance that night, as Marc Antony in *Julius Caesar*, by William Shakespeare.

As Marc Antony, Booth would speak lines horrifyingly prophetic in his case: "The evil that men do lives after them."

· · · · ·

Julia and her chaperone went backstage afterward and congratulated not only John Wilkes, but his brothers, Junius, who had played Brutus, and Edwin, who had played Cassius. The three American brothers, with John Wilkes the baby, in combination with their British father, Junius Brutus Booth, constituted what remains to this day the greatest family of tragedians in the history of the English-speaking stage.

John Wilkes gallantly kissed the hand of Julia, as though they had just met, and simultaneously slipped her a packet of chloral hydrate crystals, which would be the active ingredient in a Mickey Finn for the chaperone.

Julia had been given to believe by Booth that all she would receive from him when she came to his hotel room would be a single glass of champagne, and a single kiss she would cherish for the rest of her life after the war, back in Rhode Island, a life that would otherwise be humdrum. *Madame Bovary!*

Little did Julia suspect that Booth would mousetrap her champagne, just as *she* had mousetrapped her chaperone's beddy-bye slug of wartime white lightning, with chloral hydrate.

Ting-a-ling!

Booth knocked her up! She had never had a kid before. Something was wrong with her husband's ding-dong. She was thirty-one! The actor was twenty-four!

Incredible?

Her husband was delighted. She's pregnant? There was nothing wrong with Assistant Secretary of the Navy Elias Pembroke's ding-dong after all! Anchors aweigh!

Julia returned to Pembroke, Rhode Island, a town named in honor of an ancestor of her husband's, to have the kid. She was scared to death that the upper rims of the kid's ears would be like those of John

Wilkes Booth, pointed like a devil's, instead of curved. But the kid had normal ears. It was a boy. It was christened *Abraham Lincoln Pembroke*.

That the only descendant of the most egomaniacal and destructive villain in American history should bear that name did not become supremely ironical until, exactly two years from the night Booth ejaculated in Julia's birth canal while she was massively sedated, Booth sent a wad of lead into Lincoln's dog's breakfast, into Lincoln's brain.

At Xanadu in 2001, I asked Kilgore Trout for his ballpark opinion of John Wilkes Booth. He said Booth's performance in Ford's Theater in Washington, D.C., on the night of Good Friday, April 14th, 1865, when he shot Lincoln and then jumped from a theater box to the stage, breaking his leg, was "the sort of thing which is bound to happen whenever an actor creates his own material."

60

Julia shared her secret with no one. Did she have regrets? Of course she did, but not about love. When she turned fifty, in 1882, she founded as a memorial for her only love affair, however brief and star-crossed, without saying that's what it was, an amateur acting group, the Pembroke Mask and Wig Club.

And Abraham Lincoln Pembroke, ignorant of whose son he actually was, in 1889 founded Indian Head Mills, which became the largest textile mill in New England until 1947, when Abraham Lincoln Pembroke III locked out his striking employees and moved the company to North Carolina. Abraham Lincoln Pembroke IV subsequently sold it to an international conglomerate, which moved it to Indonesia, and he died of drink.

Not an actor in the bunch. Not a murderer in the bunch. No pixie ears.

· · · · ·

Before Abraham Lincoln Pembroke III departed the town of Pembroke for North Carolina, he knocked up an unmarried African-American housemaid, Rosemary Smith. He paid her handsomely for her silence. He was gone when his child Frank Smith was born.

Hold on to your hats!

Frank Smith has pointed ears! Frank Smith has to be one of the greatest actors in the history of amateur theatricals! He is half black, half white, and only five feet, ten inches tall. But in the summer of 2001 he gave a stunningly convincing matinee performance in the title role in the Pembroke Mask and Wig Club's production of *Abe Lincoln in Illinois,* by Robert E. Sherwood, with Kilgore Trout doing the sound effects!

The cast party afterward was a clambake on the beach at Xanadu. As in the last scene of *8 ½,* the motion picture by Federico Fellini, *tout le monde* was there, if not in person, then represented by look-alikes. Monica Pepper resembled my sister Allie. The bakemaster, a local man who is paid to stage such parties in the summertime, resembled my late publisher Seymour Lawrence (1926–1993), who rescued me from certain oblivion, from *smithereens,* by publishing *Slaughterhouse-Five,* and then bringing all my previous books back into print under his umbrella.

Kilgore Trout looked like my father.

The only sound effect Trout had to create backstage was in the last moments of the last scene of the last act of the play, of what Trout himself called "a manmade timequake." He was equipped with an antique steam whistle from the heyday of Indian Head Mills. A plumber, who was a club member and looked a lot like my brother, put the gaily mournful whistle atop a tank of compressed air, with a valve in between. That is what Trout was, too, in all he wrote: *gaily mournful.*

There were of course many club members who had no parts in *Abe*

Lincoln in Illinois, who would have liked at least to blow that big brass rooster, once they saw it and then heard it blown by the plumber himself during dress rehearsal. But the club most of all wanted Trout to feel that he was home at last, and a vital member of an extended family.

Not merely the club and the household staff at Xanadu, and the chapters of Alcoholics Anonymous and Gamblers Anonymous, which met in the ballroom there, and the battered women and children and grandparents who had found shelter there, were grateful for his healing and encouraging mantra, which made bad times a coma: *You were sick, but now you're well again, and there's work to do.* The whole world was.

61

In order that Trout not miss his cue to blow the whistle, which he was terrified of doing, of spoiling *everything* for his family, the plumber who looked like my brother stood behind him and the apparatus, his hands on Trout's old shoulders. He would squeeze those shoulders gently when it was time for Trout's debut in show biz.

The last scene in the play is set in the yards of the railroad station at Springfield, Illinois. The date is February 11th, 1861. Abraham Lincoln, in this instance played by the half-African-American great-great-grandson of John Wilkes Booth, having just been elected President of the United States in its darkest hour, is about to depart his hometown by railroad, for Washington, God help him, District of Columbia.

He says, as indeed Lincoln said: "No one, not in my situation, can appreciate my feelings of sadness at this parting. To this place, and the kindness of you people, I owe everything. I have lived here a quarter of a century, and passed from a young to an old man. Here my children have been born and one is buried. I now leave, not knowing when or whether ever I may return.

"I am called upon to assume the Presidency at a time when eleven of our sovereign states have announced their intention to secede from the Union, when threats of war increase in fierceness from day to day.

"It is a grave duty which I now face. In preparing for it, I have tried to enquire: what great principle or ideal is it that has kept this Union so long together? And I believe that it was not the mere matter of separation of the colonies from the motherland, but that sentiment in the Declaration of Independence which gave liberty to the people of this country and hope to all the world. This sentiment was the fulfillment of an ancient dream, which men have held through all time, that they might one day shake off their chains and find freedom in the brotherhood of life. We gained democracy, and now there is the question of whether it is fit to survive.

"Perhaps we have come to the dreadful day of awakening, and the dream is ended. If so, I am afraid it must be ended forever. I cannot believe that ever again will men have the opportunity we have had. Perhaps we should admit that, and concede that our ideals of liberty and equality are decadent and doomed. I have heard of an eastern monarch who once charged his wise men to invent him a sentence which would be true and appropriate in all times and situations. They presented him the words, 'And this too shall pass away.'

"That is a comforting thought in time of affliction—'And this too shall pass away.' And yet—let us believe that it is not true! Let us live to prove that we can cultivate the natural world that is about us, and the intellectual and moral world that is within us, so that we may secure an individual, social and political prosperity, whose course shall be forward, and which, while the earth endures, shall not pass away. . . .

"I commend you to the care of the Almighty, as I hope that in your prayers you will remember me. . . . Good-bye, my friends and neighbors."

An actor playing the bit part of Kavanagh, an Army officer, said, "Time to pull out, Mr. President. Better get inside the car."

Lincoln gets into the car as the crowd sings "John Brown's Body."

Another actor, cast as a brakeman, waved his lantern.

That was when Trout was supposed to blow the whistle, and he did.

As the curtain descended, there was a sob backstage. It wasn't in the playbook. It was ad lib. It was about beauty. It came from Kilgore Trout.

62

Anything we said at the cast party, the clambake on the beach, was at first hesitant and apologetic, almost as though English were our second language. We were mourning not only Lincoln, but the death of American *eloquence*.

Another look-alike there was Rosemary Smith, Mask and Wig's costume mistress, and mother of Frank Smith, its superstar. She resembled Ida Young, grandchild of slaves, who worked for us in Indianapolis when I was little. Ida Young, in combination with my uncle Alex, had as much to do with my upbringing as my parents did.

Nobody was a near double for Uncle Alex. He did not like my writing. I dedicated *The Sirens of Titan* to him, and Uncle Alex said, "I suppose the young people will like it." Nobody resembled my aunt Ella Vonnegut Stewart, a first cousin of my father's, either. She and her husband, Kerfuit, owned a bookstore in Louisville, Kentucky. They did not stock my books because they found my language obscene. So it was back then, when I was starting out.

. . . . .

Among other departed souls whom I would not summon back to life, if I had had the power to do so, but who were represented by doppelgängers: nine of my teachers at Shortridge High School, and Phoebe Hurty, who hired me in high school to write ad copy about teenage clothing for Blocks' Department Store, and my first wife Jane, and my mother, and my uncle John Rauch, husband to another of Father's first cousins. Uncle John provided me with a history of my family in America, which I printed in *Palm Sunday.*

Jane's unknowing stand-in, a pert young woman who teaches biochemistry at Rhode Island University, over at Kingston, said within my hearing, and apropos of nothing more than that day's theatrical performance and the setting sun: "I can't *wait* to see what's going to happen next."

Only the dead had doppelgängers at that party back in 2001. Arthur Garvey Ulm, poet and Resident Secretary of Xanadu, an employee of the American Academy of Arts and Letters, was short and had a big nose, like my war buddy Bernard V. O'Hare.

My wife Jill was among the living, thank goodness, and was there in the flesh, as was Knox Burger, a Cornell classmate of mine. After Western Civilization's second unsuccessful suicide attempt, Knox became a fiction editor at *Collier's,* which published five short stories every week. Knox got me a good literary agent, Colonel Kenneth Littauer, the first pilot to strafe a trench during World War One.

Trout opined, in *My Ten Years on Automatic Pilot,* incidentally, that we had better start numbering timequakes the same way we numbered World Wars and Super Bowls.

205

. . . . .

Colonel Littauer sold a dozen or more of my stories, several to Knox, making it possible for me to quit my job with General Electric and move with Jane and our then two kids to Cape Cod as a free-lance writer. When the magazines went bust because of TV, Knox became an editor of paperback originals. He published three books of mine as such: *The Sirens of Titan, Canary in a Cathouse,* and *Mother Night.*

Knox got me started, and he kept me going until he could no longer help me. And then Seymour Lawrence came to my rescue.

Also in the flesh at the clambake were five men half my age who made me want to keep on going in my sunset years because of their interest in my work. They weren't there to see me. They wanted at long last to meet Kilgore Trout. They were Robert Weide, who in this summer of 1996 is making a movie in Montreal of *Mother Night,* and Marc Leeds, who wrote and had published a witty encyclopedia of my life and work, and Asa Pieratt and Jerome Klinkowitz, who have kept my bibliography up-to-date and written essays about me as well, and Joe Petro III, numbered like a World War, who taught me how to silk-screen.

My closest business associate, Don Farber, lawyer and agent, was there with his dear wife, Anne. My closest social pal, Sidney Offit, was there. The critic John Leonard was there, and the academicians Peter Reed and Loree Rackstraw, and the photographer Cliff McCarthy, and other kind strangers too numerous to mention.

The professional actors Kevin McCarthy and Nick Nolte were there.

. . . . .

My children and grandchildren weren't there. That was OK, perfectly understandable. It wasn't my birthday, and I wasn't a guest of honor. The heroes that evening were Frank Smith and Kilgore Trout. My kids and my kids' kids had other fish to fry. Perhaps I should say my kids and my kids' kids had other lobsters and clams and oysters and potatoes and corn on the cob to steam in seaweed.

Whatever!

Get it right! Remember Uncle Carl Barus, and get it right!

63

This is not a Gothic novel. My late friend Borden Deal, a first-rate southern novelist, so southern he asked his publishers not to send review copies north of the Mason-Dixon line, also wrote Gothic novels under a feminine nom de plume. I asked him for a definition of a Gothic novel. He said, "A young woman goes into an old house and gets her pants scared off."

Borden and I were in Vienna, Austria, for a congress of PEN, the international writers' organization founded after World War One, when he told me that. We went on to talk about the German novelist Leopold von Sacher-Masoch, who in print found humiliation and pain so delectable at the end of the previous century. Because of him, modern languages have the word *masochism*.

Borden not only wrote serious novels and Gothics. He wrote country music. He had his guitar back in his hotel room, and was working, he said, on a song called "I Never Waltzed in Vienna." I miss him. I want a look-alike for Borden at the clambake, and two luckless fishermen in a little rowboat right offshore, dead ringers for the saints Stanley Laurel and Oliver Hardy.

So be it.

Borden and I mused about novelists such as Masoch and the Marquis de Sade, who had intentionally or accidentally inspired new words. *Sadism,* of course, is joy while inflicting pain on others. *Sadomasochism* means getting one's rocks off while hurting others, while being hurt by others, or while hurting oneself.

Borden said doing without those words nowadays was like trying to talk about life without words for beer or water.

The only contemporary American writer we could think of who had given us a new word, and surely not because he is a famous pervert, which he isn't, was Joseph Heller. The title of his first novel, *Catch-22,* is defined this way in my *Webster's Collegiate Dictionary:* "A problematic situation for which the only solution is denied by a circumstance inherent in the problem."

Read the book!

I told Borden what Heller said in an interview when he was asked if he feared death. Heller said he had never experienced a root-canal job. Many people he knew had. From what they told him about it, Heller said, he guessed he, too, could stand one, if he had to.

That was how he felt about death, he said.

That puts me in mind of a scene from a play of George Bernard Shaw's, his manmade timequake *Back to Methuselah*. The whole play is ten hours long! The last time it was performed in its entirety was in 1922, the year I was born.

The scene: Adam and Eve, who have been around for a long time now, are waiting at the gate of their prosperous and peaceful and beautiful farm for the annual visit from their landlord, God. During every previous visit, and there have been hundreds of them by now, they could tell Him only that everything was nice and that they were grateful.

This time, though, Adam and Eve are all keyed up, scared but proud. They have something *new* they want to talk to God about. So God shows up, genial, big and hale and hearty, like my grandfather the brewer Albert Lieber. He asks if everything is satisfactory, and thinks He knows the answer, since what He has created is as perfect as He can make it.

Adam and Eve, more in love than they have ever been before, tell Him that they like life all right, but that they would like it even better if they could know that it was going to *end* sometime.

Chicago is a better city than New York because Chicago has alleys. The garbage doesn't pile up on the sidewalks. Delivery vehicles don't block main thoroughfares.

The late American novelist Nelson Algren said to the late Chilean novelist José Donoso, when we were all teaching in the Writers' Workshop at the University of Iowa in 1966: "It must be nice to come from a country that long and narrow."

. . . . .

You think the ancient Romans were smart? Look at how dumb their numbers were. One theory of why they declined and fell is that their plumbing was lead. The root of our word *plumbing* is *plumbum,* the Latin word for "lead." Lead poisoning makes people stupid and lazy.

What's *your* excuse?

I got a sappy letter from a woman a while back. She knew I was sappy, too, which is to say a northern Democrat. She was pregnant, and she wanted to know if it was a mistake to bring an innocent little baby into a world this bad.

I replied that what made being alive almost worthwhile for me was the saints I met, people behaving unselfishly and capably. They turned up in the most unexpected places. Perhaps you, dear reader, are or can become a saint for her sweet child to meet.

I believe in original sin. I also believe in original virtue. Look around!

Xanthippe thought her husband, Socrates, was a fool. Aunt Raye thought Uncle Alex was a fool. Mother thought Father was a fool. My wife thinks I'm a fool.

I'm wild again, beguiled again, a whimpering, simpering child again. Bewitched, bothered, and bewildered am I.

And Kilgore Trout said at the clambake, with Laurel and Hardy in a rowboat only fifty yards offshore, that young people liked movies with a lot of shooting because they showed that dying didn't hurt at all, that people with guns could be thought of as "free-lance anesthetists."

He was so happy! He was so popular! He was all dolled up in the tuxedo and boiled shirt and crimson cummerbund and bow tie that had belonged to Zoltan Pepper. I stood behind him in his suite in order to tie the tie for him, just as my big brother had done for me before I myself could tie a bow tie.

There on the beach, whatever Trout said produced laughter and applause. He couldn't believe it! He said the pyramids and Stonehenge were built in a time of very feeble gravity, when boulders could be tossed around like sofa pillows, and people loved it. They begged for more. He gave them the line from "Kiss Me Again": "There is no way a beautiful woman can live up to what she looks like for any appreciable length of time. Ting-a-ling?" People told him he was as witty as Oscar Wilde!

Understand, the biggest audience this man had had before the clambake was an artillery battery, when he was a forward spotter in Europe during World War Two.

"Ting-a-ling! If this isn't nice, what is?" he exclaimed to us all.

I called back to him from the rear of the crowd: "You've been sick, Mr. Trout, but now you're well again, and there's work to do."

My lecture agent, Janet Cosby, was there.

At ten o'clock the old, long-out-of-print science fiction writer announced it was his bedtime. There was one last thing he wanted to say to us, to his *family*. Like a magician seeking a volunteer from the audience, he asked someone to stand beside him and do what he said. I held up my hand. "Me, please, me," I said.

The crowd fell quiet as I took my place to his right.

"The Universe has expanded so enormously," he said, "with the exception of the minor glitch it put us through, that light is no longer fast enough to make any trips worth taking in even the most unreasonable lengths of time. Once the fastest thing possible, they say, light now belongs in the graveyard of history, like the Pony Express.

"I now ask this human being brave enough to stand next to me to pick two twinkling points of obsolete light in the sky above us. It doesn't matter what they are, except that they must twinkle. If they don't twinkle, they are either planets or satellites. Tonight we are not interested in planets or satellites."

I picked two points of light maybe ten feet apart. One was Polaris. I have no idea what the other one was. For all I knew, it was Puke, Trout's star the size of a BB.

"Do they twinkle?" he said.

"Yes they do," I said.

"Promise?" he said.

"Cross my heart," I said.

"Excellent! Ting-a-ling!" he said. "Now then: Whatever heavenly bodies those two glints represent, it is certain that the Universe has become so rarefied that for light to go from one to the other would take thousands or millions of years. Ting-a-ling? But I now ask you to look precisely at one, and then precisely at the other."

"OK," I said, "I did it."

"It took a second, do you think?" he said.

"No more," I said.

"Even if you'd taken an hour," he said, "something would have passed between where those two heavenly bodies used to be, at, conservatively speaking, a million times the speed of light."

"What was it?" I said.

"Your awareness," he said. "That is a new quality in the Universe, which exists only because there are human beings. Physicists must from now on, when pondering the secrets of the Cosmos, factor in not only energy and matter and time, but something very new and beautiful, which is *human awareness.*"

Trout paused, ensuring with the ball of his left thumb that his upper dental plate would not slip when he said his last words to us that enchanted evening.

All was well with his teeth. This was his finale: "I have thought of a better word than *awareness,*" he said. "Let us call it *soul.*" He paused.

"Ting-a-ling?" he said.

EPILOGUE

My big and only brother Bernard, a widower for twenty-five years, died after prolonged bouts with cancers, without excruciating pain, on the morning of April 25th, 1997, at the age of eighty-two, now four days ago. He was a Senior Research Scientist Emeritus, in the Atmospheric Sciences Research Center of the State University of New York at Albany, and the father of five fine sons.

I was seventy-four. Our sister Alice would have been seventy-nine. At the time of her humbling death at the age of forty-one, I said, "What a wonderful old lady Allie would have been." No such luck.

We were luckier with Bernard. He died the beloved, sweet, funny, highly intelligent old geezer he deserved to become. He was enraptured at the very end by a collection of sayings of Albert Einstein. Example: "The most beautiful thing we can experience is the mysterious. It is the source of all true art and science." Another: "Physical concepts are free creations of the human mind, and are not, however it may seem, uniquely determined by the external world."

Most famously, Einstein is reputed to have said, "I shall never believe that God plays dice with the world." Bernard was himself so open-

215

minded about how the universe might be dealt with that he thought praying would help, possibly, in drastic situations. When his son Terry had cancer of the throat, Bernie, ever the experimentalist, prayed for his recovery. Terry indeed survived.

So it was with silver iodide, too. Bernie wondered if crystals of that substance, so like crystals of frozen water, might not teach supercooled droplets in clouds how to turn to ice, to snow. He tried it. It worked.

He spent the final decade of his professional life attempting to discredit a very old and widely respected paradigm of whence came electrical charges in thunderstorms, and where they went, and what they did and why. He was opposed. The last of the more than one hundred fifty articles he wrote, to be published posthumously, describes experiments that can demonstrate incontrovertibly whether he was right or wrong.

Either way, he could not lose. However the experiments came out, he would have found the results enormously entertaining. Either way, he would have laughed like hell.

He was funnier than I am in conversation. During the Great Depression, I learned as much about jokes while tagging after him as I did from the comedians in movies and on the radio. I was honored that he found me funny, too. It turned out that he had accumulated a small portfolio of my stuff that had amused him. One item was a letter I had written to our uncle Alex when I was twenty-five. At that time, I had published nothing, had a wife and son, and had just come from Chicago to work as a flack for General Electric in Schenectady, New York.

I got that job because Bernie had become a celebrity in the GE Research Laboratory, in association with Irving Langmuir and Vincent Schaefer, for experiments with cloud seeding, and because the company decided to have regular newspaper people handle its publicity. At Bernie's suggestion, GE hired me away from the Chicago City News Bureau, where I had been a beat reporter. I had worked simultaneously for a master's degree in anthropology at the University of Chicago.

I thought Uncle Alex knew that Bernie and I were at GE then, and that I was in Publicity. He *didn't* know!

And Uncle Alex had seen a syndicated photograph of Bernie, credited to the *Schenectady Gazette*. He wrote to that paper, saying he was "a wee bit proud" of his nephew and would like a copy of the picture. He enclosed a dollar. The *Gazette* got the picture from GE, and so forwarded the request to my new employer. My new boss, logically enough, handed it on to me.

I replied as follows on blue GE stationery:

GENERAL ELECTRIC

COMPANY

GENERAL OFFICE SCHENECTADY, N. Y.

1 River Road
Schenectady 5, N. Y.

November 28, 1947

Mr. Alex Vonnegut
701 Guaranty Building
Indianapolis 4, Indiana

Dear Mr. Vonnegut,

    Mr. Edward Themak, city editor for the SCHENECTADY GAZETTE, has referred your letter of November 26th to me.

    The photograph of General Electric's Dr. Bernard Vonnegut originated from our office. However, we have no more prints in our files, and the negative is in the hands of the United States Signal Corps. Moreover, we have a lot more to do than piddle with penny-ante requests like yours.

    We do have some other photographs of the poor man's Steinmetz, and I may send them to you in my own sweet time. But do not rush me. "Wee bit proud," indeed! Ha! Vonnegut! Ha! <u>This office made your nephew, and we can break him in a minute -- like a egg shell</u>. So don't get in an uproar if you don't get the pictures in a week or two.

    Also -- one dollar to the General Electric Company is as the proverbial fart in a wind storm. Here it is back. Don't blow it all in one place.

Very truly yours,

Guy Fawkes

Press Section
GENERAL NEWS BUREAU

Guy Fawkes:bc

As you can see, I signed it "Guy Fawkes," a name infamous in British history.

Uncle Alex was so insulted that he flipped his wig. He took the letter to a lawyer to find out what legal steps he might take to compel an abject apology from someone high in the company, and to make this cost the author his job. He was going to write to the President of GE, telling him he had an employee who did not know the value of a dollar.

Before he could take such steps, though, somebody told him who Guy Fawkes was in history, and where I was, and that the letter was so hilariously grotesque that it had to be a joke from me. He wanted to kill me for making such a fool of him. I don't think he ever forgave me, although all I intended was that he be tickled pink.

If he had sent my letter to General Electric, demanding spiritual restitution, I would have been fired. I don't know what would then have become of me and my wife and son. Nor would I ever have come upon the material for my novels *Player Piano* and *Cat's Cradle*, and several short stories.

Uncle Alex gave Bernie the Guy Fawkes letter. Bernie on his deathbed gave it to me. Otherwise, it would have been lost forever. But there it is.

Timequake! I am back in 1947 again, having just come to work for General Electric, and a rerun begins. We all have to do again exactly what we did the first time through, for good or ill.

Extenuating circumstance to be mentioned on Judgment Day: We never asked to be born in the first place.

I was the baby of the family. Now I don't have anybody to show off for anymore.

．　．　．　．　．

A woman who knew Bernie for only the last ten days of his life, in the hospice at St. Peter's Hospital in Albany, described his manners while dying as "courtly" and "elegant." What a brother!

What a language.